This book belongs to:

....

....

....

OXFORD CHILDREN'S MYTHS AND LEGENDS

Stories from England
Stories from Ireland
Stories from Scotland
Stories from Wales

OXFORD CHILDREN'S MYTHS AND LEGENDS

GWYN JONES

— ❖ —

STORIES FROM
WALES

OXFORD

UNIVERSITY PRESS

OXFORD
UNIVERSITY PRESS

Great Clarendon Street, Oxford OX2 6DP

Oxford University Press is a department of the University of Oxford.
It furthers the University's objective of excellence in research, scholarship,
and education by publishing worldwide in

Oxford   New York

Auckland   Cape Town   Dar es Salaam   Hong Kong   Karachi
Kuala Lumpur   Madrid   Melbourne   Mexico City   Nairobi
New Delhi   Shanghai   Taipei   Toronto

With offices in

Argentina   Austria   Brazil   Chile   Czech Republic   France   Greece
Guatemala   Hungary   Italy   Japan   Poland   Portugal   Singapore
South Korea   Switzerland   Thailand   Turkey   Ukraine   Vietnam

Oxford is a registered trade mark of Oxford University Press
in the UK and in certain other countries

First published as *Welsh Legends and Folk-tales* 1955
First published in this paperback edition 2013

British Library Cataloguing in Publication Data

Data available

ISBN: 978-0-1 9-273663-5

1 3 5 7 9 10 8 6 4 2

Printed in Great Britain

Paper used in the production of this book is a natural,
recyclable product made from wood grown in sustainable forests.
The manufacturing process conforms to the environmental
regulations of the country of origin

I Blant
pa le bynnag y bônt

ACKNOWLEDGEMENT

For permission to adapt for some of the stories
in this volume parts of our translation of the *Mabinogion*
(Golden Cockerel Press, 1948; Everyman's Library, 1949)
I am most grateful to my friend and colleague Thomas Jones.

CONTENTS

THE FOUR
BRANCHES
OF STORY

PWYLL AND PRYDERI

I

The Marriage of Pwyll and Rhiannon

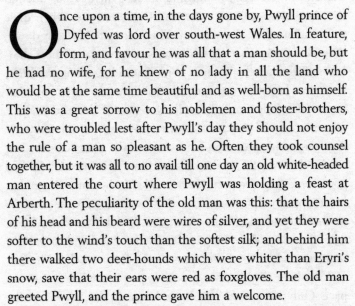

Once upon a time, in the days gone by, Pwyll prince of Dyfed was lord over south-west Wales. In feature, form, and favour he was all that a man should be, but he had no wife, for he knew of no lady in all the land who would be at the same time beautiful and as well-born as himself. This was a great sorrow to his noblemen and foster-brothers, who were troubled lest after Pwyll's day they should not enjoy the rule of a man so pleasant as he. Often they took counsel together, but it was all to no avail till one day an old white-headed man entered the court where Pwyll was holding a feast at Arberth. The peculiarity of the old man was this: that the hairs of his head and his beard were wires of silver, and yet they were softer to the wind's touch than the softest silk; and behind him there walked two deer-hounds which were whiter than Eryri's snow, save that their ears were red as foxgloves. The old man greeted Pwyll, and the prince gave him a welcome.

'Lord,' said the old man, 'I marvel to see you here at Arberth, and yet you have not gone to the top of the green mound which stands behind your court.'

'Why,' asked Pwyll, 'what is the quality of the mound, that I should profit by climbing it?'

'The quality of the mound is this,' answered the old man, 'that when the son of a true king sits upon its summit, either he shall receive a blow and a wound or he shall see the marvel he desires most in all the world.'

'I am not afraid of a blow or a wound,' said Pwyll. 'As for the marvel, I should be glad to see that.'

So he and the old man, with the two hounds at their heels, and followed by the noblemen of the court, left the court and walked to the green mound, and because the day was hot and the mound steep they were glad to sit and rest when once they had reached the summit. The moment Pwyll sat down, they saw a lady on a big white horse, with a garment of shining gold-brocaded silk upon her, come riding along the highway that led past the mound. 'Is there any one here that knows this lady?' asked Pwyll. Not one of them, they said. 'Then let one of you go to discover her name and condition.' A young nobleman arose and went to the road to meet her, but by the time he reached the bottom of the mound she had gone some distance past. He hurried after her, but though her horse appeared to move at a slow walking-pace he saw her getting further and further from him. Quickly he took a horse from the court, the most mettlesome he could find, and drove in his spurs, but the faster he rode the further behind he fell, and the lady all this time appearing to proceed at a walking-pace. Only too quickly his horse began to flag, and when he noticed this he reined in and returned to the mound and informed Pwyll of his discomfiture.

'Be easy, lad,' said Pwyll, 'there is some magic meaning here, and only the old man can inform us of it.' But when he turned to speak with him, there was no old man to be seen, and no dogs either, the very ground and sky quite empty of them, and the leashes and the collars gone too. 'There is only one thing to be done,' said Pwyll at that. 'For tonight we will return to the court, but tomorrow at the same time we will come to sit on the mound and trust to see this marvel again.'

So they did, and at the appointed time went to the mound to sit down. 'Lad,' said Pwyll to the young man who had gone after the rider the day before, 'bring with you the swiftest horse you know to be in our meadows.' He did so and stood waiting with the horse as the company sat down. That same moment they saw the lady coming along the road at the same ambling pace. 'Be ready, lad,' Pwyll warned him, and when he was fully ready he said: 'Now ride and find out who she is.' But even as the lad mounted his horse she had passed him by, and by the time he was settled in his saddle there was a clear space between them. He now put his horse into an amble, and when this did not help him he gave his horse the reins. All the time she was proceeding at the same unhurried pace as before. Next he gave his horse the spurs and drove it till it was white with lather, but if anything she now seemed even further ahead. His horse began to flag, so he reined in and returned to the mound and told Pwyll how he had failed the second time.

'I see now,' said Pwyll, 'that it is idle for anyone to pursue her save myself. And yet I know she has an errand to this plain, if only she could be brought to declare it. However, for the present we will return to the court.'

They did this, and spent the night in song and carousal, and on the morrow they beguiled the day until it was time to go to the mound.

'Groom,' said Pwyll, 'saddle my best horse and bring him to the roadside, and fetch too my best stirrups and my spurs.' He did so, and the company ascended the mound and sat down. That same moment they could see the lady coming along the same road, on the same horse and in the same guise, and at the same ambling pace as they had seen her yesterday. 'Groom,' said Pwyll, 'I see the rider. Give me my horse.' He mounted his horse, but even as his foot entered the stirrup the lady passed him by. He turned after her, and gave his horse the reins, feeling sure that at the second bound or the third he would catch up with her; but though he was soon driving his horse to its utmost speed, and she in no haste at all, he could not close a hoof-breadth of the space that lay between them.

'Ah, maiden,' cried Pwyll then, 'for the sake of him you love best, stay for me a while.'

At his words the maiden stayed and waited. 'Gladly,' she replied. 'And you would have been kinder to your horse had you asked this long since.'

'Lady,' said Pwyll, 'I am a king in this country, but it is not for that reason I ask you these questions. Where have you come from, and where are you going?'

'I travel to please myself,' said the maiden. 'And I am pleased to see you, lord.'

She drew back that part of her head-dress which covered her face, and it seemed to Pwyll that the countenance of every maiden he had ever seen was unlovely compared with hers. 'My welcome to you in Dyfed,' he said. 'Will you tell me who you are?'

'I am Rhiannon, daughter of Hefeydd the Old, and they want to give me to a husband against my will. But I will not have him unless you yourself reject me, for you are he I love most of men. And it was to hear your answer to this that I came riding here.'

'Between me and heaven,' said Pwyll joyfully, 'I have a quick and ready answer, for had I the choice of all the ladies and maidens in the world, you are the maiden I would choose.'

'Then make a tryst with me,' said Rhiannon, 'a year from tonight, at the court of my father Hefeydd. I will have a feast prepared against your coming, and at that feast you shall ask for me at my father's hand. And now I must go my way.'

They parted, she to her father's court, and he to meet his war-band on the mound. But when the year wore on to the appointed time he set off a-wooing with his men, and they were a hundred armed noblemen together. They came to Hefeydd's court and asked for Rhiannon, and Pwyll's suit had a joyous answer. There had been great preparations made against his coming, and all the resources of the court were dispensed at his direction. The hall was now made ready, and they went to table, Pwyll in the seat of honour, Hefeydd the Old on one side of him, and Rhiannon on the other, and the rest of the company thereafter according to their rank.

The carousal had begun, and their mirth was at its highest when Pwyll saw enter a tall, auburn-haired youth of royal mien, wearing a cloak of gold-brocaded silk and shoes of red leather. He came boldly into the hall and greeted Pwyll in a full, clear voice.

'My welcome to you, friend,' replied Pwyll. 'Sit where your rank will have it, and drink with us and be merry.'

'There is a time for all things, lord. Know that I am a suitor come here to ask a boon of you.'

7

'Friend,' said Pwyll, 'you are the first to ask a boon at my hand this day. Ask what you will, for the day's sake, and it shall be yours.'

But Rhiannon had caught at his arm. 'Alas, lord,' she cried in dismay, 'this is a sorry answer of yours!' And the noblemen and ladies of the court cried out with her, lamenting Pwyll's rash answer.

'Why, lady,' asked Pwyll, 'what have I done?'

'Lord,' said the auburn-haired youth, 'what you have done is to pledge your word in the hearing of the whole court. Shall I name my request?'

'Name it,' said the troubled Pwyll.

'Tonight you think to marry the lady whom I love best. It is to ask for her, and the feast and the preparations that are here, that I have come.'

Pwyll sat dumb, without word or whisper from his lips. 'You may well sit dumb,' said Rhiannon, 'and it would have been kinder to us both had you sat dumb long since.'

'I did not know who he was,' pleaded Pwyll. 'Indeed, I still do not know.'

'Who else but the man to whom they wanted to give me against my will? For this is Gwawl son of Clud, a chieftain strong in hosts and dominions, and since you have spoken the way you have, bestow me on him without more delay, lest he carry away your honour with your broken word.'

'Alas,' said Pwyll, 'what kind of counsel is this? I can never bring myself to do so hateful a deed.'

The lady Rhiannon leaned nearer to Pwyll and her voice sank to a whisper. 'Do as I say, and all will yet be well. Take this small bag and keep it safe: that is the first thing. Promise him what is yours to promise, but you cannot give him the feast and the preparations that are here, for they are not yours, but mine: that is the second. And after that be dumb again, and leave the rest of the talk to me.'

'Lord,' said Gwawl impatiently, 'it is time I had my answer. Will you speak now?'

'What is mine,' said Pwyll, 'you shall have—and that is the lady Rhiannon. But the feast and the preparations are not mine, and I may not bestow them on you.'

'Friend Gwawl,' added Rhiannon, 'they are already bestowed upon the men of Dyfed and the war-band of my father's court. But return again, a year from tonight, and a feast shall be prepared for you in your turn, and at that feast you shall make me your wife, if you so desire.'

Gwawl set off instantly for his domain, to prepare his whole kingdom for this marriage. But Pwyll had much talk with Rhiannon before he left for his main court in Dyfed.

A year passed, and at its ending Gwawl set out and a great retinue with him, and came to the feast which had been prepared for him at the court of Hefeydd the Old. Pwyll set out too, and the men of Dyfed, a hundred all told, and they came together to an orchard near the court, where his men took shelter. Pwyll clad himself in coarse, shabby garments, and wore big rag boots on his feet, so that when he entered the hall as the carousal began he must shuffle over the floor like any beggar. He came forward to the seat of honour and gave Gwawl greeting, and called down God's blessing on all the company.

'My welcome to you, friend,' said Gwawl. 'Sit where you may, and drink and be merry.'

'There is a time for all things, lord. Know that I am a suitor come here to ask a boon of you.'

'I welcome your request, friend,' Gwawl was pleased to answer. 'And if it is a fair request, saving only my men and the lady Rhiannon, you shall have it gladly.'

'Judge whether it is fair, lord. I would not ask it save to ward off hunger and want. The boon is that this small bag should be filled with food for me.'

'Men,' said Gwawl to his attendants, 'fill this bag, and fill it with all that is best of meat and drink.'

The attendants went bustling to and fro with wine and meat and bread, but despite all that went into the bag it seemed no fuller than before.

'Why, friend,' asked Gwawl, raising his eyebrows, 'will your bag ever be full?'

'Lord,' said the beggar (for such they thought him in the court), 'it is the peculiarity of this bag that it will never be full until a true prince who sits with his bride shall arise and tread down the provisions in the bag with both his feet, at the same time proclaiming so that all men may hear: "Enough is now in this bag, so shut it!"'

'Brave sir,' said Rhiannon, where she sat next to Gwawl at table, 'there is no one can do this except you. Arise now quickly.'

At her bidding Gwawl arose from the table and put his two feet inside the bag. 'Enough is now in this bag,' he said loudly, 'so shut it!'

The words were still between his tongue and his teeth when Pwyll pulled up the bag so that Gwawl was head over neck inside it. The words were still between his teeth and his lips when Pwyll closed the bag and knotted its thongs, and blew a blast on his horn. The blast was still in the mouth of the horn when down came his war-band, descending upon the court and seizing Gwawl's host and throwing each of them into his own captivity. As the first man entered, Pwyll threw off his old rag boots, and as the last entered he stood before them in his own princely array. And each man as he came inside struck the bag a sharp blow, and, 'What is here?' he asked. And the man who preceded him made answer: 'A badger!' 'Why,' asked old Hefeydd, 'what game are you playing now?' 'The game of Badger in the Bag,' they told him. And that was the first time that anyone played Badger in the Bag in the Island of Britain.

'Lord,' cried the man from the bag, 'if you will hear me— this is not the death for me, to be killed in a bag.'

'He is right,' said the joyful Pwyll, 'nor would it be proper to do him more hurt on this my wedding day.'

So they let Gwawl out of the bag, and took oaths of him that he would never seek vengeance for what had happened, nor lay claim in all his life to anything of Pwyll's or Rhiannon's. Then, these oaths taken, they released all his men, and they were given baths and ointments and healing balms, and that same day they set off for their own domain. And the dust had not yellowed their horses' hooves when Pwyll married Rhiannon, and the hall was arrayed afresh for their wedding-feast.

On the morrow they arose in the young of the day and travelled towards Dyfed, and when they reached Arberth there was a great feast prepared in readiness for them. As soon as their coming was known, the full muster of the land was gathered to give them greeting, and not a nobleman or noble-man's wife left Rhiannon without receiving a sparkling brooch or ring or precious jewel as the first gift from her bounty. And so it came about that they ruled the land in friendship and prosperity that year and in peace and tranquillity the next.

II
The Birth of Pryderi

———— ❖ ————

But later it happened, in the third year of the marriage of Pwyll and Rhiannon, that the people of the land came to feel great heaviness of heart because the throne of Dyfed was still without an heir. 'Lord,' they said, 'we are much troubled lest after your day we shall not enjoy the rule of so pleasant a man as you. Truth to tell, you cannot last for ever, and it is our advice that you set aside the wife you have and take another by whom you may have a son to follow you.'

'There is a time for all things, friends,' Pwyll reproved them, 'and many a chance may yet befall. Let us put off this talk for a twelvemonth and a day, and maybe I shall then submit to your counsel.'

Before the end of that time a son was born to Pwyll and Rhiannon, and all the countryside offered up prayers and rejoicing. The night he was born six women were brought into the queen's chamber at Arberth, to keep watch over the mother and child. For the first part of the night they kept good watch, but towards midnight they grew drowsy, and soon they were all asleep. It was cockcrow when they awoke, and when they looked in the place where they had laid the boy to sleep, there was no sign of him. 'Alas,' they cried, 'the boy is lost, and our lives shall be forfeit unless we find him.' They sat down to think what might be done in the matter, and this is what they decided on. In the chamber near the bed there was a couched stag-hound and her pups, so they agreed to kill some of the pups and smear the blood on Rhiannon's face and hands, and throw the bones before her, and swear that she herself had destroyed her son. 'For we are six to one,' they said, 'and she will be helpless against our insistence.'

No sooner had they agreed to this than the lady Rhiannon awoke. 'Ladies,' she asked, 'where is my son? I cannot wait to see him.'

'Alas,' they said, 'lady, do not ask us for your son. Look, we are black and blue from struggling with you, and in all our lives we never saw a woman of such strength and violence as you. We did what we could, but it was to no purpose, and it is best that you should hear at once the crime you have committed. Lady, you have destroyed your son.'

The lady Rhiannon knew well that they were lying. 'Poor creatures,' she said, 'it is your fear that makes you accuse me. Take my promise that I will protect you if you tell the truth.'

'Faith,' they replied, 'it is not for us to suffer hurt for your sake, queen and lady though you are. We say again that you destroyed your son last night.'

'Poor wretches,' she said a second time, 'it would be far better for me to know the truth.' But for all her words, whether fair-spoken or pitiful, she received the same answer from the women as before.

Then Pwyll arose, and his war-band and the hosts, and the

disaster which had befallen the kingdom was made known to them. The chief men assembled together, and they urged Pwyll that he should set Rhiannon aside, or have her put to death, because she had wrought so monstrous a crime. But the answer they received from Pwyll was this. 'Once before you asked me to set aside my wife, and time proved you wrong. I think it will prove you wrong again. I will not put her away, and the only punishment she shall suffer is that which our law enjoins for a case unproved.'

'Then let her do penance,' said the nobles. 'We will be content with that.'

And because Rhiannon preferred doing penance to wrangling with the women, and because the women were resolute in their lie, she took on her a penance. This was to remain in that court at Arberth till the end of seven years, and to sit every day near the horse-block which was outside the gate, and to relate her story to every newcomer who might be expected not to know it; and to everyone who would permit her to do so, she must offer to carry guest and stranger on her back to the court. And in this fashion the years passed by.

At this same time the lord Teyrnon was ruler over Gwent Is-Coed. There was no better man alive than he. He had a great treasure in his house, by way of a mare; she was the handsomest mare in the kingdom. Every May-eve she dropped a foal, but what became of it no one knew. One night (and it was the very night that Rhiannon's son was born) Teyrnon talked this over with his wife. 'It is very slack of us,' he reminded her, 'to let our mare foal each year and have never a foal to show for her pains. Tonight is May-eve, and shame on my beard if I do not discover what evil destiny it is that snatches away the colts.'

He had the mare brought inside the building, and with his sword about him he settled down to watch for the night. Early in the night the mare cast a colt which was unusually large and handsome, and strong enough to stand up on the spot. Teyrnon rose to his feet and was remarking the sturdiness and good colouring of the colt when he heard a great commotion, and after the commotion he saw a huge claw coming in through the window of the house and seizing the colt by the mane. Teyrnon instantly drew his sword and took aim at the claw, and struck off the arm at the elbow, so that that much of the arm together with the colt fell back inside the house with him. A loud scream instantly mingled with the commotion, and he flung open the door and rushed outside, but because the night was black and starless he saw nothing to pursue. Besides, he remembered that he had left the house open behind him, and thought it prudent to return. And there at the door he found an infant boy in swaddling clothes, with a sheet of brocaded silk wrapped round him. He took up the boy, marvelling, and carried him in to his wife.

'Lady,' he asked, 'are you asleep?'

'I was asleep,' she made answer, 'but I awoke as you came in.'

'Wife,' he said, 'we have always wanted a son, and now, if you will have him, here is a boy for us.' He went on to tell her the whole story, and her heart grew tender towards the child, and they knew by the sheet of brocaded silk and by the white-ness of his skin that he was the son of gentlefolk. 'Shall we keep him as our own child, wife?' Teyrnon asked her.

She took the child in her arms and laid him in the bed

beside her. 'Between me and heaven,' said Teyrnon's wife, 'from this day on we have a son indeed.'

The very next day they had the boy baptized with the baptism that was then practised, and he was called Gwri Goldhair, because the hair that was on him was yellow as gold. For three years he was reared in the court with Teyrnon, and by that time was as big as a child twice his age. By the end of his fourth year he was bargaining with the grooms of the horses to let him take the beasts to water; and it was then that Teyrnon gave him the colt which he rescued on the same night he found the boy, and the boy grew perfected in horsemanship till few in the kingdom were so skilful as he.

By this time they had heard news of Rhiannon and her penance, and one day as Teyrnon was watching the boy ride it came into his head and heart that he had never seen a lad more likely to be the son of Pwyll prince of Dyfed. He carried his mind back to the night when he found him, and realized that it was the selfsame night that Rhiannon suffered her sad loss. Grief and anger seized him together: grief that he must lose the son he loved so well, and anger for the punishment that was wrongly inflicted upon Rhiannon. As soon as he was alone with his wife he told her his thoughts, and they agreed that whatever their own grief and deprivation, they would know no happiness till they restored the boy to his rightful parents. No later than the morrow Teyrnon equipped himself, with two more horsemen, and the boy as a fourth along with them, upon the horse which Teyrnon had given him. They rode off and it was not long before they reached Arberth. As they drew near to the court they could see a woman sitting beside the horse-block. 'Shame on my beard,' said Teyrnon, 'if

I let this wickedness last beyond today.' They cantered on to the court, and soon they were abreast of her.

'Chieftain,' said Rhiannon, 'I pray you ride no further. I must carry each one of you to the court, for that is my penance for slaying my son with my own hands and destroying him.'

'Queen and lady,' said Teyrnon, 'I do not think any man of mine will go upon your back.'

'Go who will,' vowed the boy, 'I shall not go.'

'No more will we,' said Teyrnon.

They went on to the court, and there was great joy at their coming. Soon the joy was even greater, as Pwyll returned from a progress through Dyfed. They went to wash and then into the hall, and Pwyll made Teyrnon welcome. And before they began the carousal Teyrnon told Pwyll of his adventure with the mare and the boy, and how the boy had been taken for their own by himself and his wife, and how they had reared him and taught him horsemanship. 'Send for Rhiannon,' he requested Pwyll. 'Her grief is greater than ours can ever be.' And when she entered, 'Lady,' said Teyrnon, 'see there your son. Lying and wrong have been practised upon you. And I believe,' he added, 'that there is no one in all this company who will not recognize that the boy is Pwyll's son.'

'If this were so,' said Rhiannon, 'I should now be delivered of all my care.'

'Lady,' said the chieftain Pendaran Dyfed, 'with that word you named your son: Pryderi son of Pwyll [Care or Thought, son of Understanding]; no other name could so become him.'

'And yet,' said the gracious Rhiannon, 'perhaps the name he has already may suit him better.'

'What name is that?' asked Pendaran Dyfed.

'Gwri Gold-hair was the name we gave him,' said Teyrnon.

'No,' said Pendaran Dyfed, 'his name shall be Pryderi.'

'It is only right,' Pwyll admitted, 'that his name should be taken from the word his mother spoke when she received glad tidings of him.'

On this they all agreed, and Pwyll swore everlasting friendship with Teyrnon, and for Teyrnon's wife he and Rhiannon chose gifts of beauty and price, and above all they sent her their love and gratitude. The boy was given in fosterage to Pendaran Dyfed, and soon Teyrnon returned to his own domain, and every great man who had a home elsewhere went back to it.

So the years ran by, and Pryderi son of Pwyll was raised with fitting care until he became the most gallant youth, and the handsomest and the best skilled in manly pursuits of any in the kingdom. And so it continued till there came an end to the life of Pwyll prince of Dyfed and he died. And then Pryderi took the kingdom, and ruled over it prosperously, and was beloved by his people and by all who came near him. And it was then that he married Cigfa daughter of Gwyn, a man descended from the high-born princes of this Island.

THE STORY OF BRANWEN

———— ❖ ————

At the time when Pryderi was lord over Dyfed, Brân the Blest was king over the whole Island of Britain. He had one sister, the princess Branwen; and Manawydan was his full brother. In addition, he had two half-brothers on the mother's side. One of these was Nisien, who brought friendship to men and peace to contending armies. The other was Efnisien, the greatest quarreller that ever lived in Britain. It was mirth to him to cause strife between his brothers, even when they were most loving together.

It happened one day that Brân was seated with his brothers and noblemen on the great rock of Harlech, and as they sat there in the sunshine, looking out to sea, they spied thirteen ships coming from the south of Ireland. They had the wind behind them, and advanced with an easy, swift motion, so that they quickly neared the land.

'I see ships,' said the King, 'making boldly for my land. Brother,' he told Manawydan, 'I should like you to go and enquire as to their purpose.'

Manawydan at once set off with Nisien and a troop of men to await them at the haven. As the ships drew near, they told each other that they had never in all their lives seen ships of fairer rig or handsomer tackle than these, with their coloured sails and standards of bright brocaded silk. Suddenly one of the ships drew ahead of the others, and they could see a painted shield lifted high above the ship's deck, with its point held uppermost in token of peace. Manawydan too lifted his shield, and men put off in small boats from the Irish ship, and soon their voices might be heard across the water. King Brân heard them too, for the sound was borne upwards to the high rock where he waited far above their heads.

'God prosper you,' the King greeted the newcomers, 'and a peaceful welcome to you. Whose are the ships, and who is your lord?'

'King,' they replied, 'these are the ships of Matholwch, King of Ireland. He has an errand to you.'

'What errand is that?' asked Brân.

'He has come in person to ask for Branwen your sister in marriage. Will you bid him land?'

'Land he shall,' replied the King. 'I am willing for that. And later we will take counsel concerning his request.'

The boats returned with this message, and Matholwch came to greet Brân, and all that day and night there was a joyous gathering of the two hosts, both those of Ireland and those of the Island of Britain. In the morning the kings and their great men took counsel together, and it was agreed that Matholwch should marry Branwen, so that there might be peace from that time forth between the kingdoms. Of all maidens in the world Branwen was loveliest; and she was one of the Three Great Ladies of this Island.

The marriage feast was set for Aberffraw, and the hosts at once departed for that place, Matholwch and his host in their ships, but Brân and his men by land. No greater feast was ever held in this Island, though for a good reason it was not held within a house. There was no house so big that it might contain the godlike Brân, so they had to carouse in their tents, and when the carousal was over it was in tents that they slept.

In the morning the officers of the court had to arrange for the billeting of the horses and their grooms, and they found billets for them from the mountains as far as to the sea. It was as they were completing this task that Efnisien, the quarrelsome brother, arrived from a journey he had made into the south.

He recognized neither grooms nor horses, and, 'Whose horses are these?' he asked fiercely.

'These are the horses of Matholwch, King of Ireland,' an officer told him.

'Then what are they doing here?'

'They are here because Matholwch himself is here. He has married your sister Branwen, and the marriage feast was held last night.'

'What?' cried Efnisien. 'Have they done this with a maiden so noble as she, giving her in marriage without full consent of all her brothers? They would not have insulted me so had I been the basest groom of the stable! I shall be revenged on the Irishman for this.'

With that he drove off the grooms and set upon the horses, and like a madman he beat and spoiled them till they were fit for nothing about a royal court.

News of this quickly reached Matholwch, where he rested in his tent. 'Lord,' said his noblemen, 'a great insult has been laid upon you, and it was done not by accident but by intent.'

'I find it strange,' he answered, 'that they should have given me the maiden Branwen for my wife, if their purpose was to insult me.'

'Lord,' they said, 'do not forget that you too are a king. There is no choice for you now but to go to your ships.'

But they could not be so silent that word of their going was not brought to King Brân, who at once sent messengers to know the reason for such discourtesy. When they returned, the King was much moved by their recital.

'Go back again,' he ordered, 'and tell Matholwch that the insult put upon him is an even greater affront to me. Tell him too that the offender is my brother on the mother's side, so that I may not kill or destroy him. Tell him further that he shall have a sound horse for each of those spoiled, and that I will give him for his pride a staff of silver which shall be as thick as his little finger and as tall as himself, and a plate of red gold as broad as his face. And if this does not content him, then let him come to see me face to face, and Nisien shall make peace between us on those terms which he himself shall name. For I will not have him go to Ireland in anger, lest it bring sorrow on Branwen.'

The messengers went after Matholwch, and his men were not yet fully embarked. They gave him their message in so friendly a fashion that he thought it best to accept Brân's offer. 'Besides,' thought the Irish, 'if we reject it, and anger the King, we may well come by greater hurt from him than from Efnisien.' So they furled their opening sails, left the ships tethered there, and returned to the court.

Once more the pavilions and tents were arranged for them as though they had been an immense hall, and they sat down to eat and drink. Once more Brân and Matholwch began to converse together. But though Matholwch was informed of the reparation to be paid him, he seemed to his neighbour to have grown listless and sad. 'Why, man,' said Brân, 'you are not such a good talker tonight as you were last night. If you think our reparation too small, speak up, and have it increased just as you will. You need wait no longer than tomorrow for the horses.' But because Matholwch's thanks were still too few, he continued: 'And I will enhance the reparation in a way you have not dreamed of. Tomorrow, when the counting of horses is done, I will give you the cauldron whose name is the Cauldron of Rebirth. Its virtue is this, that if one of your men is slain today, cast him into the cauldron, and by tomorrow he will be as good a man as ever, except that he will not be able to speak.'

'With that,' said Matholwch, 'I may well be content.'

For what was left of the night he was merry enough, and in the morning his horses were made over to him, so many that they must travel from district to district for horses till the tally was complete. And then, when their count was ended, Bran gave him the Cauldron of Rebirth, which all men reckoned one of the chief treasures ever to be found in the Island of Britain.

The next day Matholwch set out with his thirteen ships for Ireland; and aboard the swiftest of them, on a dais spread with red brocaded silk, sat Branwen his wife on a throne of red gold and ivory. Horns and trumpets blew merrily from sea to shore and out to sea again, but it was observed of Brân that long after the ships were out of sight he walked the shore with slow, sad steps, and that there were tears in his eyes.

'Brother and King,' said the wise Manawydan, 'does one weep on a wedding day?'

'Fear not, Brân,' added Nisien. 'All living things beyond the sea will love our sister Branwen.'

'If not,' threatened the fierce Efnisien, 'we will cross over and destroy Ireland.'

But Brân shook his head sadly, and knew only grief and foreboding. But he said nothing to the others as yet, and soon they left the darkened beach for the tents.

In Ireland there was great joy at the coming of Matholwch and Branwen, and not an Irishman but was proud that his King had found the fairest maiden in the world to honour his throne. All the noblemen and their ladies came to visit her, and when they took their leave they carried with them some sparkling brooch or ring or precious stone as their first gift from the Queen's bounty. For one whole year she lived in honour and friendship among them, and when her son Gwern was born, their joy knew no limit. And to Branwen too her happiness seemed great as mortal may endure.

But in the second year there was first a murmuring and then a loud complaint in Ireland, when men remembered the insult laid on Matholwch in Wales, and the maiming of his horses. Soon his foster-brothers and others of his court began to taunt him with cowardice, in that he had taken payment for his injury and not exacted fierce vengeance. Then the men of his host threatened to rise in rebellion against him unless he avenged this disgrace. 'For a king's shame is the shame of his warriors too,' they complained. It thus happened that the king was persuaded to banish Branwen from the royal apartments; and next she was sent to cook for the court; and every day when the butcher had finished cutting up the meat he would seek her out and give her a hard box on the ear. And all this time she was not permitted to see her son Gwern.

'Lord,' his men advised Matholwch, 'it would be prudent to set a ban on the ships and the ferries and the coracles, and on all boats that ply to Wales. And all the boats that come to us from Wales, have their crews set in your deepest prison, and then Brân and the men of the Island of the Mighty shall never know what has become of Branwen.'

For three years it continued thus. But meantime Branwen reared a starling on the end of her kneading-trough, teaching it human speech, and instructing it how it might recognize her brother Brân. Then she wrote a letter which told of the sorrows and the dishonour that were upon her, and when she had secured this under the root of the starling's wings, she sent it over the sea to Wales. The bird reached this Island, and flew on to Caer Seint in Arfon, and recognized Brân as he gave out justice at an assembly of his there one day. Straightway it alighted on his shoulder, and as it ruffled its feathers men could see the letter, and knew that the bird had been reared in a human dwelling.

Then Brân took the letter and read it, and to the starling in reward he gave a bowl for food and a bowl for water and a perch in every royal palace throughout his dominions. A heavy sorrow weighed upon him for his sister and for the affliction that would now come upon the men of the Island of the Mighty. First he assembled his warriors and read to them the letter, and then he and his hosts took counsel. When they decided to set out for Ireland, every man save Efnisien wore a troubled brow. But Efnisien showed his teeth in a thin smile and was for ever sharpening his spear and his axe and his

27

sword. Seven knights were left behind to guard the kingdom, and Cradawg son of Brân was their leader.

When the hosts were ready they sailed for Ireland. At that time the sea between Wales and Ireland was neither deep nor wide; for it was later that the waters overflowed the Three Drowned Kingdoms. There was no ship so big that it might contain the godlike Brân, so he crossed over by wading, and carried all the string minstrelsy safe and dry on his back.

It happened about this time that Matholwch's swineherds had gone down to the seashore and were attending to their swine. 'Why,' they cried, 'what a wondrous sight is over the sea!' Driving their swine before them, and with a great barking of dogs, they hurried off to tell Matholwch what they had seen.

'Lord,' they said, 'we have wondrous news of a wondrous sight. We have just seen a forest growing out of the sea.'

'That is wondrous indeed,' Matholwch made answer. 'But was that all you saw?'

'That was the least of it, lord,' they assured him. 'For alongside the forest we saw a big mountain, and it was moving, and there was a lofty ridge on it, and a lake on each side of the ridge; and the ridge and the lakes were moving too.'

'Well,' said the King, 'I see no one here who is capable of explaining that. But perhaps Branwen will know what it is.' And he sent messengers to the kitchen to ask her.

'Lady,' they said, when they had described what the swineherds had seen, 'do you know what this is?'

'You mock me when you call me lady,' said the gentle Branwen, 'but even so I will tell you what it is. These are the men of the Island of the Mighty, who have heard of my sorrows and affliction, and are coming to Ireland to avenge the wrong done to me.'

'Alas, lady,' they said to this, 'and what was the forest that grew out of the sea?'

'The masts of ships and their yards,' she told them.

'Alas then, lady, what was the mountain that might be seen alongside the ships?'

'Brân the Blest, my brother,' she told them, 'who comes here wading.'

'Alas, lady, and again alas,' they begged, 'then what was the lofty ridge on the mountain, and what were the lakes on each side of the ridge?'

'My brother is angry,' she replied, 'as he looks towards Ireland. The two lakes are his eyes, one on each side of his nose.'

They returned to Matholwch with what they had learned, and all the fighting men of Ireland and the warriors of every headland were mustered in haste, and counsel taken among the hosts. 'There is only one thing we can do,' advised his chief noblemen. 'We must withdraw across the river Shannon, and break down the bridge. There are loadstones at the bottom of the river, which prevent any ship or vessel from sailing along it.' And this was their plan: they retreated across the river and broke down the bridge.

Soon Brân approached land and his fleet with him, and they made for the bank of the Shannon.

'Lord,' said the wise Manawydan, 'I know the peculiarity of this river. No ship or vessel can sail along it, and there is now no whole bridge across it. What is your plan concerning a bridge?'

'There is only one plan,' said Brân. 'He who is chief, let him be a bridge. I will myself be a bridge.'

This was the first time that saying was uttered, and it is still a proverb among the men of Britain. Then he lay down across the river, and hurdles were placed upon him, and his hosts passed through over him.

At this sight, terror and dismay spread among the Irishmen, and even as he was rising up there came messengers from Matholwch, bearing friendly greetings and offering that the kingdom should be given into the hand of Gwern, Brân's sister's son, as reparation for the wrong and shame done to Branwen. All that Matholwch asked for himself, they said, was that Brân might make provision for him, either in Ireland or in his own land.

'If I do not take the kingdom myself,' replied Brân, 'I may follow this counsel. But you need not tell your lord that I am other than angry with him.'

The messengers returned and urged Matholwch to find a better answer. 'There is only one thing you can do,' advised his chief noblemen. 'There has never been a house so big that it might contain Brân. Therefore make a house in his honour, so that he and his men may be contained in the one half of it, and you and your men in the other. And when you are all inside the house, offer him the kingship and do him homage, and then one of two things will happen. Either he will repay you the honour you have done him by building a house as big, and make peace with you on terms you would yourself desire, or we shall plan a ruse to undo him.'

The King thought this wisdom, and sent messengers again to Brân, and at the request of Branwen, who feared lest the land should be laid waste, Brân granted the Irish a truce.

The terms of truce were drawn up, and the house was built

big and roomy. Now the ruse the Irishmen planned was this, to fix a peg on either side of every pillar of the hundred pillars that were in the house, and to fix a hide bag on every peg, and in every bag there should be an armed man waiting. But it was all to no purpose, for it happened that the quarrelsome Efnisien came in ahead of the host of the Island of the Mighty, scanning the house with fierce, ruthless looks, and looking for some cause of offence.

'What is in this bag?' he asked, pointing with his iron forefinger.

'Flour, friend,' said an Irishman nervously.

'Then this will not hurt him,' retorted Efnisien, and he felt about the bag till he found a head, and then squeezed the head till he felt his fingers sink through bone into brain. 'And what have we here?' he asked, leaving that one, and setting his hand on another.

'Flour, friend,' said the Irishman, with a grimace.

'Then he will bear kneading,' retorted Efnisien, and he played the same trick on him and on all of them, until of the two hundred men in the bags he had left alive but one. 'And what have we here?' he asked, coming to set his hand on the bag.

'Flour, friend,' said the Irishman, with a groan. By this time Efnisien's fingers were tiring, and as he squeezed the last head he could tell that there was armour on it. Even so he did not leave him till he was dead, and then he sang a verse:

> *'Each of these bags held flour, so they say,*
> *Or flower of warriors, gallant and gay;*
> *But flour in a bag or flower in array,*
> *With flour and flower I've now done away.'*

Hardly had his voice fallen silent before the two hosts came into the house and filled it, the men of Ireland on the one side, and the men of the Island of the Mighty on the other. As soon as they were seated there was concord between them, and the kingship of Ireland was bestowed on the boy Gwern. And then, when peace was concluded, the godlike Brân called the boy to him; and from Brân he went to the wise Manawydan, and from Manawydan to Nisien the peace-maker; and as he walked between them and his mother, all who saw him loved him. All, that is, save one man, and that man Efnisien.

'Why,' cried Efnisien in his iron voice, 'comes not my nephew, my sister's son, to me? Am I less in his sight than my other brothers? Is he grown so proud now that he is King of Ireland? I would gladly show love to the boy.'

'Go, boy,' said Brân, 'and have no fear. He is your uncle, your mother's brother, even as I am.' And the boy laughed and went to him gladly.

'Now,' said Efnisien in his heart, 'an enormity the whole world would not think might be committed is the enormity I shall now commit.'

And because his heart was black with hatred of Matholwch the boy's father, he arose and caught up the boy by the feet, and before anyone there might lay hold of him he thrust the boy headlong into the blazing fire. And when the gentle Branwen saw her son burning in the fire, she made as if to leap after him from the place where she was sitting between her two brothers. But Brân grasped her with one hand, and his shield with the other, as the two hosts rose up throughout the house; and as each man snatched at his arms, Brân the Blest supported Branwen between his shield and his shoulder, and for all the rage of men, the tumult and the fighting, no hurt came to her save the hurt that must break her heart.

Quickly the Irish kindled a fire under the Cauldron of Rebirth, and as their own men fell they flung them into the cauldron till it was full, and on the morrow they stepped out as good fighting men as ever, except that they were unable to speak. When Efnisien saw this, and saw too that there was no room in the cauldron for his own countrymen, 'Alas', he said in his heart, 'woe is me that I should have caused this pile of dead of the Island of the Mighty. And shame on my beard,' he said, 'if I seek no remedy for it.' He crept in among the dead bodies of the Irish, and soon two bare-legged Irishmen came along and flung him into the cauldron as though he was one of themselves. Then he stretched himself out in the cauldron, so that the cauldron burst into four pieces, and his heart burst also.

Had it not been for this, none of the men of the Island of the Mighty would have survived. Brân himself was wounded in the foot with a poisoned spear. Because he knew his hurt to be mortal, he commanded Manawydan to strike off his head. 'And take the head,' he bade them, 'and carry it to the White Mount in London, where you must bury it with its face towards France. You will be a long time upon the road before you reach there.

'In Harlech first you will be feasting for seven years, with the birds of Rhiannon singing to you; and all this time you will find my head as pleasant company to you as ever you found it when I was still your lord and friend.

'Then at Gwales in Penfro [Grassholm in Pembrokeshire] you will dwell in happiness for fourscore years; and until you open the door towards Aber Henfelen, on the side facing

Cornwall, you may remain there, and the head with you uncorrupted. But once that door is opened, you shall remain no longer, but make for London to bury the head. And now, when my head is off, you must cross over to the other side.'

Then his head was struck off by the sad Manawydan, and the seven survivors set off for the other side, taking the head with them, and Branwen too, the eighth in their company. They came to land at Aber Alaw in Talebolion, in their own beloved country, and there they sat down to rest. And Branwen looked on Ireland and the Island of the Mighty, all that she might see of them. 'Alas, Son of God,' she said, 'woe is me that ever I was born! Two good islands have been laid waste because of me.' And she heaved a great sigh and broke her heart. And a four-sided grave was made for her, and she was buried there on the bank of the Alaw.

These were the seven men who came alive from Ireland: Manawydan son of Llŷr, and Pryderi lord of Dyfed; Glifieu, and Ynawg, and Taliesin Chief of Bards; Gruddieu son of Muriel, and the rash Heilyn son of Gwyn the Old.

'It will be best now,' they said, 'that we follow our lord's counsel and proceed to Harlech.'

Soon, as they journeyed, they met with a troop of men and women coming towards them. 'Have you news?' asked Manawydan. 'No news,' they said, 'no news at all, save that Caswallawn son of Beli has conquered the Island of the Mighty and is now a crowned king in London.'

'What has become of Cradawg son of Brân,' they asked, 'and each of the men we left behind to guard the kingdom?'

'Caswallawn fell upon them suddenly and slew the six men; and Cradawg broke his heart with grief and consternation to see a sword slaying his men, and no one brandishing it. Caswallawn was apparelled in a magic mantle, so that no one might see him slay the men, but only the sword flashing in air.'

Then they went on to Harlech, and there they sat down and began to regale themselves with meat and drink. Even as they started to eat and drink there came three birds, who sang to them a certain song, and all the songs they had ever heard were hard and unlovely compared with that. Far, far out over the sea they must look to discern them, and yet the song was as clear as if the birds had been close at hand. And there they stayed feasting for seven years.

Then, at the end of the seventh year, they set out for Gwales in Penfro, and found a great royal hall there overlooking the sea, and went inside, and found two doors standing open, but the third door, which faced Cornwall, stood closed. 'Our lord spoke truth,' said Manawydan. 'That is the door we must not open.' From that night forth they lived there without stint and were joyful. And despite the sorrows they had beheld before their eyes, and all those ills they had themselves endured, there came to them no remembrance of that or any other sorrow in the world. And they passed fourscore years there, and they did not remember a time more joyous or delightful, nor could any of them tell by his fellows that it was so long a time. And all the while the head was as pleasant company to them as when their lord had been with them alive. And because of those fourscore years their sojourn there was called the Assembly of the Wondrous Head.

Then, at the end of the fourscore years, this is what Heilyn son of Gwyn did one day. 'Shame on my beard,' he said, 'if I do not open the door to know whether it is true what Brân said concerning it.' He opened the door, and his eyes beheld Cornwall and Aber Henfelen. As he did so, they grew conscious of every loss they had ever sustained, and of the deaths of their kinsmen and friends, and of every sorrow that had ever befallen them, and all these things as sharply as if they were even then befalling; and above all else they felt the loss of their lord. From that same moment they knew no rest, and set out with the head towards London, and however long the way before them, they reached there at last, and buried the head in the White Mount. When it was buried, that was one of the Three Happy Concealments of this Island, and one of the Three Unhappy Disclosures when it was disclosed; for such was the virtue of the head, that no plague could come across the sea to Britain while it remained in its concealment.

That was the adventure of the seven men who set forth from Ireland with their lives. And that is how this story ends, concerning the blow to Branwen, which was one of the Three Unhappy Blows in this Island; and concerning the Assembly of Brân, when the hosts of seven-score districts and fourteen went over to Ireland to avenge the blow to Branwen; and concerning the feasting in Harlech for seven years, and the singing of the birds of Rhiannon, and the Assembly of the Head for fourscore years.

THE TRIALS OF DYFED

———— ❖ ————

When the seven men who escaped alive from Ireland had buried the head of Brân the Blest their lord in the White Mount in London, with its face towards France, Manawydan, Brân's brother, looked upon the town and on his companions, and heaved a great sigh, and felt much grief and longing within him. 'Alas,' he said, 'woe is me, that there is no one save us in the whole kingdom without a place to rest this night.'

'Lord,' said Pryderi, for he too was one of those seven men, 'it will not help us to be unhappy. Your cousin Caswallawn is King in the Island of the Mighty, and though he has done you wrong, and more wrong than me, yet you have never been greedy after land or territory. Are you not one of the Three Ungrasping Chieftains?'

'True,' admitted Manawydan, 'but it saddens me to see another man in my brother's place, and it is not to be thought that I will live in the same house with him.'

'I know a plan for that,' Pryderi told him. 'The seven districts of Dyfed are still under my sway; my mother Rhiannon has charge of them till my return, and my wife Cigfa lives there and helps her. Now, let us return to Dyfed, and I will bestow my mother upon you in marriage. When she was in her bloom of years there was no lovelier lady, and indeed there is no lovelier lady alive this day. Besides, I know that you will never have listened to better converse than hers, which exceeds that of other women even as the singing of her birds is more beautiful than that of all the feathered nations of the air.'

'My heart grows tender towards her,' said Manawydan, 'and we will go to Dyfed.'

They set out on their way, the two of them together, without other company, and though the road was long and hard they reached Dyfed at last. News of their coming had reached Rhiannon and Cigfa, and the two ladies prepared a splendid feast for them, and as they sat and feasted and began the carousal it seemed to Manawydan that he had never heard a lady converse so well as Rhiannon, or beheld any so graced with beauty as she. His grief fell from him, and, 'Lord,' he said to Pryderi, 'I would gladly adopt the counsel you offered me in London.'

'What counsel was that?' asked Rhiannon.

'That I might bestow you, lady, in marriage upon this royal man, if you and he agree.'

'I agree,' said Rhiannon, smiling.

'I too agree,' said Manawydan. And before the feast ended he married her.

When the feast was ended they began to make a progress through Dyfed, and to hunt and take their pleasure. And as they wandered the countryside they thought they had never seen a land more delightful to live in, nor a better hunting ground for stag and boar, nor a land more abundant in honey and fish. Such great friendship grew up between the four of them that none wished to be without the other, by night or by day. But soon Pryderi must go again into England, and at Oxford he tendered his homage to Caswallawn son of Beli, and Caswallawn confirmed him in the lordship of Dyfed. He made no long stay in England, and the joy of his friends knew no bounds when he returned.

One day they held a feast at Arberth, and they were beginning the carousal when there came into the hall an old, white-headed man whose hair and beard were as wind-blown silver and who led with him on silver chains two deer-hounds which were whiter than Eryri's snow, save that their ears were red as foxgloves. The old man greeted Pryderi, and the prince gave him a welcome.

'Lord,' said the old man, 'I marvel to see you here at Arberth and yet you have not gone to the top of the green mound which stands behind your court.'

'Why,' asked Pryderi, 'what is the quality of the mound, that I should profit by climbing it?'

'The quality of the mound is this, that when the son of a true king sits upon its summit, either he shall receive a deadly hurt and sorrow or he shall see the marvel he desires most in all the world.'

'Son,' said Rhiannon, 'there is some magic meaning here, and it would be folly in a happy prince to sit on that mound.'

'I am not afraid of hurt and sorrow,' replied Pryderi. 'As for the marvel, I should be glad to see that.'

'If Pryderi goes,' vowed Manawydan, 'I shall go with him and our fate shall be as one.'

It thus happened that the four of them arose and proceeded to Gorsedd Arberth with many noblemen about them. But when they sought to speak further with the old man, lo and behold, he was not to be seen, and no dogs either, the very ground and sky quite empty of them, and the chains and the collars gone too. 'Well,' said Pryderi, 'we will sit just the same.' And as they were sitting thus, lo, there came a peal of thunder, and with the magnitude of the peal a fall of mist coming, so that no one of them could see the other. And after the mist, lo, every place was filled with light. But when they looked to where they were used to see the flocks and the herds and the dwellings, not a thing could they see: neither house nor beast nor smoke nor fire nor man nor dwelling, but the houses of the court empty, desolate, uninhabited, without man, without beast within them, their very companions lost, without their knowing anything of them, save they four only.

'Alas,' cried Manawydan, 'where is the host of the court, and our friends and company too?' Into the hall they came: not a soul was there. Into bower and sleeping-chamber they went: not a soul could they see. In mead-cellar and in kitchen there was nothing but desolation.

From that day forth they began to wander the land, seeking to descry house or habitation, but all they could find were birds and wild beasts. When their victuals came to an end they began to live on the meat they hunted and on fish and the honey of wild swarms. In this fashion they passed a whole year, and then a second, but in the third year they grew weary.

'Faith,' said Manawydan, and he spoke for them all, 'we cannot continue like this. We had better go into England and seek some craft with which to make a living.'

So they set off for England, and the town they came to was

Hereford, where they began to make saddles for horses. So skilled was Manawydan at working in leather and staining it with blue-azure, that so long as he had goods to sell, no pommel or saddle save his was bought throughout all Hereford. Soon the other saddlers of the town found that they were losing their profit, and it was not long before they decided to kill Manawydan and his companion Pryderi, if there was no other way of getting rid of them. However, news of this came to Pryderi's ears and he discussed with Manawydan what they should do.

'My advice,' said Pryderi, 'is that we should fall upon the villeins and kill them all.'

'Not so,' said the wise Manawydan. 'Even if we killed them, and not they us, we should surely be caught and put in prison. It would be much better for us to go to another town and seek a new living.'

The four of them set off for Ludlow, where they began to make shields for warriors. So skilled was Manawydan at cutting out leather and staining it even as he had stained the saddles, that so long as men might buy their shields from him, there was no other shield-maker in the town might take a silver penny. He was brisk, too, and made shields without number, and no long time passed before their fellow-townsmen grew angry and plotted to kill him and his companion, if there was no other way of getting rid of him.

'We will not take such wrong and insult from the villeins,' said Pryderi. 'My advice is that we waylay them and kill them all.'

'Not so,' answered the wise Manawydan. 'Even if we were to succeed in that, Caswallawn would hear of it, and we should certainly come to grief. I think it best that we go to another town.'

This time they went to Gloucester, where they began to make shoes for the citizens. It was by Manawydan's advice that they did this, for he thought that there was less courage in shoemakers than in the makers of saddles and shields, and that the shoemakers of Gloucester would not have the heart to molest them. By his advice too they bought only the finest leathers for soles, and he found out the best goldsmith in the town and ordered him to make buckles and gild them with pure gold, and when he had looked on at the work for a short time, he grew more skilled in the craft than the goldsmith himself. That was why he was called one of the Three Gold Shoemakers. In Gloucester, as elsewhere, so long as he had a shoe or a high boot to sell, no one would buy from any other shoemaker throughout the town, and it was not long before they plotted together to kill the companions.

'Ah,' said Pryderi, 'why should we take this from such thieving villeins? Let us face them and kill them all.'

'Not so,' said the wise Manawydan. 'We should gain nothing but disfavour and imprisonment if we did so kill them. No, Pryderi. We have outlived our welcome in England, and it will be best for us to return again to Dyfed.'

Here too he spoke for them all. With joy in their hearts they set out for their own country, and though the road was long and hard they came to Arberth at last. They kindled fire and collected dogs, and once more they went hunting and caught fish and took honey from the swarms, until they had been home for a whole year.

One morning Pryderi and Manawydan rose up in the

young of the day to hunt. Some of their dogs ran on ahead of them, making for a small copse which grew near the court. But no sooner had they run into the copse than they ran out again, their backs bristling with fear, and came cringing towards the men. 'Come,' said Pryderi, 'we must see what has frightened them in the copse.' They were still a short way from it when a huge boar all silver-white rose up out of the copse to confront them. The dogs, hollaed on by the men, attacked him rather timorously, and he did not fall back till the men drew near. Several times he did this, standing at bay against the dogs, who did not dare close with him, and falling back before the men, till at last they found themselves on the green mound and could see a fortress before them, in a place where they had never seen stone or building before. And as the dogs ran barking forward, the boar withdrew into the fortress, and the dogs rushed yelping after him. From the top of the mound the two men watched and listened, marvelling meanwhile at the fortress, but though they stood there a long time they saw and heard nothing.

'Lord,' said Pryderi, 'I shall wait no longer but enter the fortress to seek my dogs.'

'Not so,' advised Manawydan, 'it would be folly for you to enter a place we have never seen before. There is some magic meaning here, and I suspect that it is the same hand that cast a spell over Dyfed that has now caused this fortress to appear.'

'The more reason to seek it out,' answered Pryderi. 'Besides, I will not abandon my dogs.'

Despite all Manawydan's warnings he walked towards the fortress and went inside. Even so, neither boar nor dogs could he see, nor any sign of habitation. But in the middle of the fortress floor he saw a fountain with marble work around it, and on the fountain's edge a golden bowl fastened to four chains, and this upon a marble slab, and the chains ascending into the air without any end or limit. He was so transported with the beauty of the gold and the fine workmanship of the bowl that he stepped forward to lay hold of it. But the moment he laid hold of it, his two hands stuck fast to the bowl and his feet to the marble slab on which he was standing, and his power of speech forsook him, so that he could not utter one word. And so he remained, silent and still in the middle of the fortress.

Outside, in the eye of the sun, Manawydan waited for him till late into the afternoon. Then, because he was convinced that he would get no tidings of Pryderi or his dogs, he went sorrowfully back to the court.

'I see your face changed,' said Rhiannon. 'You have bad news of my son?'

'It is not good news, lady.'

She cried out in alarm at that. 'Where is your friend, and where are his dogs? He was not the man in all his life to abandon his dogs.'

'Lady,' he told her, 'hear my story.' And he told it in every detail.

'Ah, lord,' she reproached him, 'you have proved yourself a bad comrade to him you have lost, though he was the best of comrades to you.'

'Lady,' he asked her, 'would you be better pleased had neither of us returned?'

But she had no ear for his words as she hurried out in the direction where he had told her she would find the fortress.

As she reached the mound she saw it, and saw it clearly, for there was no concealment on it, and its gate stood open. Instantly she made towards it and entered through the gate, and there in the middle of the floor she could see Pryderi laying hold of the bowl. 'Alas, son,' she reproached him, 'was it to lay hold of this bowl that you have brought such fright upon us?' She took hold of the bowl herself, to remove it from his grasp, but the moment she laid hold on it her hands stuck to the bowl and her feet to the slab, and she in her turn was unable to utter one word. And then, as day turned to night, there came a peal of thunder in the air over them, and a fall of mist descending, and between the peal and the mist the fortress vanished, and mother and son vanished too.

When Pryderi's wife Cigfa learned that there was no one left in Dyfed save Manawydan and herself, she made a loud outcry that she had as soon die as live without her husband.

'Lady,' Manawydan assured her, 'your grief is no greater than mine. It may even be less in that I am older and have less time to hope for restitution. Have no fear, for in me you see the truest comrade lady ever had, and I shall do all things for your comfort for so long as it pleases heaven to keep us in this affliction.'

She thanked him for his words. 'But we cannot stay thus,' she told him. 'What would be good counsel for us, do you think, lord?'

'We have lost our dogs,' he said. 'We have no means of living here. Let us go once more into England, where I may practise a craft.'

'What craft shall that be?' she asked him. 'Let it be a clean one, I beg of you.'

'I will be a shoemaker,' he told her, 'as I was before.'

45

'Lord,' she said, 'I cannot commend that for its cleanliness, but you must have your way.'

He began his craft at Gloucester in England, and this time again he fashioned his shoes from the finest leathers to be bought in the town, and he buckled the shoes with gold buckles as before, so that the work of every other shoemaker in the town was judged paltry and mean compared with the beauty and neatness of Manawydan's. So long as he had a shoe or high boot to sell, not a silver penny was paid to any man else, till the shoemakers grew jealous of him and plotted to kill him. This reached Cigfa's ears, and, 'Lord,' she said, 'is this to be suffered from such baseborn villeins? Take your sword in place of your awl and kill them.'

'That was Pryderi's counsel too,' he warned her. 'Not so. Let us return to Dyfed.'

Straightway they did so. Now when Manawydan set out for Dyfed he carried with him a burden of wheat on his shoulders, and it was with him still when they reached Arberth. He at once began to hunt that same countryside he had hunted before with Pryderi, and because he had no dogs he grew skilful at catching fish and trapping wild animals in the coverts. He began to till the ground too, and in season he sowed a croft, and a second, and a third, and with the sun and dew upon them the wheat sprang up throughout the crofts, so that no man alive had ever seen finer wheat than that.

He watched out the seasons of the year, till the harvest was at hand. He came to look at the first of his crofts and found it ripe. 'I will reap this tomorrow,' he told himself. He returned that night to Arberth, and on the morrow in the grey of the dawn he came with scythe and sickle, intending to reap the croft. But to his amazement all he found left was the stalks, naked after each one of them had been broken off where the ear grows from the stalk, and the ears carried away, and the stalks left there all bare.

For a time he stood shaking his head, between surprise and dismay. Then he came to look at the second croft, and that too was ripe. 'I will reap this tomorrow,' he told himself. And on the morrow in the green of the dawn he came with scythe and sickle, reckoning to reap the croft. But once more all he found was naked stalks, and every ear of corn carried away, so that the ground was empty of them. 'Alas,' he lamented, 'who is it that wishes to complete my ruin?' And he told himself that it must be he who had earlier begun it, and had ruined Dyfed as well.

He came to look at the third croft. 'No man alive,' he vowed, 'has seen finer wheat than this, and it is fully ripe. Shame on my beard if I do not keep watch this night to see who is robbing me.'

He took up his arms and began to watch the croft. Towards midnight he heard a great squeaking and rustling and looked anxiously about him. Because his eyes had grown used to the dark, he could see the mightiest host of mice in the world, with no measure or limit set to their number, and each mouse squeaking and rustling as it ran to the croft. In a trice they were inside the croft and each of them climbing up along a stalk and bending it down under its weight, and making off with the ears of wheat and leaving the stalks all naked. For all he could see, there was not one single stalk without a mouse to it, and each of them running off, and the ears with them.

In wrath and anger he rushed in among the mice to try and catch them. But he could no more keep an eye on one of them than on the gnats in the air. He missed once, he missed twice; he missed a dozen, he missed a score; and all this time the mice were running before him and carrying off the ears. Then he espied a mouse which was very big and heavy, so that he judged it incapable of any fleetness of foot. He marked it down and went after it, and because it was slow and clumsy in its movements, he caught it and put it in his glove, and tied up the mouth of the glove with a string so that it might not get out. At this the other mice fled with squeaks of dismay, and soon there was silence throughout the croft. Tired and angry, Manawydan walked home with his glove.

Cigfa was seated in the hall when he came in. She watched him brighten the fire and hang the glove by its string on a peg. 'What have you there, lord?' she asked him.

'A thief,' he replied, 'whom I found thieving from my croft.'

'What kind of a thief does one put inside one's glove, lord?' she asked him.

'Hear the whole story,' he replied. And he told it to her in every detail, how the crofts had been laid waste for him, and how the mice came squeaking and rustling to the third croft in front of his eyes. 'But this one mouse was heavy and big, so I caught it, and tomorrow shame on my beard if I do not hang it.'

'Lord,' she said, 'are you sure it is seemly for a man of your rank and dignity to go hanging such a creature as that?'

'Believe me, lady,' he retorted, 'I would hang them all, had I caught them!'

'Well, lord,' she told him, 'there is no reason why I should succour the creature except to keep you clear of shame. Hang it, if you must.'

'My thanks to you, lady,' said Manawydan. 'That is what I intend to do.'

'For my part, so you may,' she replied, and with that last word went to her bed.

On the morrow, towards mid-morning, Manawydan made for Gorsedd Arberth, taking the mouse with him. There he erected two forks on the highest point of the mound. While he was about this, he suddenly saw coming towards him a clerk, clad in old and threadbare garments. He paused for a long time and stared at him, for it was now seven years since he had set eyes on man or beast there, except for those four who had been together till two of them were lost.

'Lord,' said the clerk, 'good-day to you.'

'Good-day to you, too,' replied Manawydan. 'Where do you come from, clerk?'

'From song-making in England, lord. Why do you ask?'

'There is a reason for everything,' said Manawydan.

'I am just passing by towards my own country, lord. What kind of work are you engaged upon, may I ask, lord?'

'I am hanging a thief.'

'What kind of a thief, lord? The creature in your hand looks like a mouse to me, and it ill becomes a man of such rank and dignity as yours to touch any such thing as that. Let it go, lord.'

'Not I,' said Manawydan. 'I caught it thieving, and I will execute upon it the law concerning a thief and hang it.'

'Lord,' said the clerk, 'I should be sorry to see a man of your dignity so degrade himself. I have a pound here which I received as alms in England. Now take the pound and let the creature go.'

'Not I,' said Manawydan. 'I will neither free it nor sell it.'

'As you please, lord. Were it not so unseemly to see a man of your dignity handling such a creature I should not have spoken.' And away went the clerk.

Manawydan now proceeded to fix the crossbeam upon the forks, but as he was about this he suddenly saw coming towards him a priest on a richly caparisoned horse.

'Lord,' said the priest, 'good-day to you.'

'Good-day to you too,' replied Manawydan. 'Have I your blessing?'

'The blessing of God be upon you. What kind of work are you busied about, may I ask, lord?'

'I am hanging a thief.'

'What kind of a thief, lord?'

'A thief in the shape of a mouse. I caught it thieving, and it must suffer the doom of a thief.'

'Lord,' said the priest, 'lest your dignity be sullied by handling such a creature, I will gladly redeem it. So let it go, lord.'

'Not I. I will neither sell nor let it go.'

'True enough, lord,' said the priest, 'it has no legal price upon it. But for your rank's sake I will give you three pounds, so let it go!'

'Shame on my beard,' said Manawydan, 'if I want anything for this mouse save its due, and that is to hang it.'

'For my part, lord, do your pleasure.' Away went the priest.

Manawydan now noosed the string about the neck of the mouse, but just as he was drawing it up he suddenly saw coming towards him a bishop's retinue, with loads of baggage and a great train, and the bishop himself hurrying to meet him. So for one reason and another he stayed his work.

'Lord,' said the bishop, 'what kind of work is yours?'

'I am hanging a thief.'

'But is it not a mouse,' said the bishop, 'which I see in your hand?'

'Aye,' replied Manawydan, 'but mouse as she is, she is a thief too.'

'Why,' said the bishop, 'since I have come by at the hour of this creature's destruction, it will be my good deed to redeem it. Lest a man of your dignity should be seen destroying such a poor creature as that, I had rather pay seven English pounds. So take the money and let her go.'

'Not I,' said Manawydan.

'Then if you will not let her go for seven, take twenty-four English pounds. Only let her go!'

'Not I,' said Manawydan.

'Then take twice twenty-four, and all the horses you see on this plain, and the loads of baggage, and the great train. Only let her go!'

'Not I,' said Manawydan.

'Then name your price,' said the bishop.

'Gladly,' said Manawydan. 'And the price I name is that Rhiannon and Pryderi shall be set free.'

'That you shall have. Now let the mouse go free.'

'Not till I have more than that. The charm and the enchantment must be removed from Dyfed.'

'Gladly. But let the mouse go!'

'Not yet,' vowed Manawydan. 'I must first know who the mouse is.'

'She is my wife. Ah, lord, as one of the Three Compassionate Chieftains, I beg you to let her go.'

'Why did she come as a thief to my croft?' asked Manawydan.

'Ease the string,' the bishop pleaded, 'and I will tell you. I am Llwyd son of Cil Coed, and it was I who through my friendship with Gwawl son of Clud cast the enchantment over Dyfed. I took vengeance on Pryderi for the game of Badger in the Bag which his father Pwyll played on my friend at the court of Hefeydd the Old. Later, when we knew that you were a dweller in this land, my war-band came to ask me to transform them into mice, so that they might destroy your corn. It was they who came the first night and the second and destroyed your two crofts. The third night my wife came to me too, with the ladies of the court, that they might take part in the vengeance, and them also I transformed. But my wife was with child, and that was why you were able to overtake her and put her in your glove. Because you did so, I have come here to meet you. I will give you Rhiannon and Pryderi, and I will remove the charm and the enchantment from Dyfed. And now that I have told you who she is, why, lord, let her go.'

'Not till I have your promise that no vengeance shall ever be taken for this upon Rhiannon and Pryderi.' And he added: 'Or upon me either.'

'You shall have that,' promised Llwyd, 'and you have asked more wisely than you know. I had a shrewd stroke waiting for you all, had you forgotten.'

'Aye,' said the wise Manawydan, 'that was why I asked.'

'And now,' invited Llwyd, 'set my wife free for me.'

'Only when I see Rhiannon and Pryderi stand before me without bonds,' said Manawydan.

'Look where they come!' cried Llwyd. 'Please let her go.'

At that moment and in that place Rhiannon and Pryderi appeared before him, and Manawydan greeted them, and they embraced and sat down together.

'Good sir,' cried Llwyd son of Cil Coed, 'now that you have received all that you knew how to demand, set my wife free for me.'

'Gladly,' said Manawydan. And she was set free, and her husband struck her with a magic wand, and she changed back into the most beautiful young woman that any of them had ever seen.

'Look around you upon Dyfed,' Llwyd told them, 'and you will see the folk and the houses and all the habitations as they were when at their best.' And so it was, and they saw the land inhabited once more, complete with its herds and its flocks and its dwellings. And when Llwyd and his wife had gone away to their own country, Manawydan led Rhiannon and Pryderi to where Cigfa awaited them at Arberth, and they lived there together in prosperity for many a golden year.

LLEU AND THE FLOWERFACE

In those far-off days when Math son of Mathonwy was lord over Gwynedd, there lived at his court and served him one who was still more of a magician than he. This was his nephew Gwydion son of Dôn, the man who made the circuit of Gwynedd on his behalf and ruled his war-band. It was the same Gwydion who by magic and strength slew Pryderi lord of Dyfed at Maentwrog in north Wales, after carrying off his pigs.

It happened one day when Gwydion was lying in his bed of a morning, half-awake, half-asleep, that he heard a low cry from the chest he kept at his bed's foot. In a moment or two he heard it again, though no cry could ever be quieter. Quickly he stepped out of bed and went to open the chest, and when he had done so, he could see an infant boy lying there in a silken sheet, thrusting his arms through its folds and spreading it apart. He lifted the boy out of the chest and carried him to the light, and it seemed to Gwydion that there was something of his own likeness in the boy's face. 'Shame on my beard,' said Gwydion, 'if I do not maintain him as well as myself.' That same day he found a woman to look after the boy, and the boy throve so well that in a year's time one would have remarked on his size had he been twice that age. By the end of his second year he was big and sturdy enough to be sent to the court, and Gwydion received him there and loved him as his own son, and the boy loved Gwydion and called him father, and all who saw them said that there was never such likeness or such love between any other two in the Island of Britain.

Still the boy throve, and so quickly that by the time he was four years old one would have remarked on his size had he been eight. It was now that Gwydion set off one day, and the boy with him, and made his way on foot to the castle of the lady Aranrhod. When they entered the court there, the lady rose up to meet him, to make him welcome and to give him greeting.

'Heaven prosper you, lord,' she said. 'You do not come as often as you used to do.'

'There is a reason for everything,' said Gwydion. 'Heaven prosper you too, lady.'

'But who,' she asked, 'is the lad who follows you, and bears your likeness in his face?'

'Lady,' said Gwydion, 'this is your son.'

'Alas, man,' cried Aranrhod, 'why bring such shame upon me as to say he is my son!' And she hid her face in her hands, so great was the shame that possessed her.

'Lady,' replied Gwydion, 'unless you suffer a greater shame than that I should rear so fine a lad as this, your shame is no great thing. Take him now at my hands.'

'What is his name?' asked Aranrhod. 'For without a name he is no son of mine, no son of thine, and no kinsman of the king's.'

'Faith,' said Gwydion, 'as yet he has no name. Do you name him, lady.'

At this the lady Aranrhod smiled more with her teeth than her eyes. 'No,' she said, 'there is no hope that I will name him. Moreover, I will swear on him a destiny that he shall never get a name unless he gets it from me.'

'Wicked woman,' cried Gwydion in a rage, 'to treat your own son thus! But never fear,' he added more quietly, setting his hand on his son's shoulder, 'he shall have a name, and sooner than you think.' And with that they turned away from the court and went back to Caer Dathyl to spend the night, the boy in sleep, but Gwydion in deep thought and meditation.

On the morrow in the young of the day Gwydion arose and took his son with him and they went walking along the seashore between there and Aber Menai. Wherever he saw dulse and sea-girdle on the rocks he collected them, and made a ship from them by magic; and wherever he saw seaweed and dulse on the sands those too he collected, and from them he made cordwain. Next he put colours on the cordwain till no one in the world had seen leathers so lovely. He set a sail in the ship, and he and the boy sailed on till they reached the sea-gate of Caer Aranrhod, where they at once began cutting out shoes and stitching them. Watchmen saw them from the castle tower, and as soon as Gwydion knew that they were overlooked he took away their own proper semblance and put another semblance upon them, so that they would not be recognized.

'What men are they in the ship?' asked Aranrhod.

'Shoemakers,' they told her.

'I have need of shoes. Go and see what leathers they have, and what kind of work they do.'

When the messengers reached the ship, Gwydion was colouring cordwain in gold. They returned and told Aranrhod that they had never seen leathers so lovely and stitching so true.

'Take the measure of my foot,' she ordered, 'and ask the shoemaker to make shoes for me.'

Gwydion fashioned the shoes, but he cut them much bigger than the measure.

'These are the best shoes in the world,' said Aranrhod, 'and he shall be paid for them. But they are too big. Let him make me shoes that are smaller.'

Gwydion fashioned the shoes, but this time he cut them much smaller than the measure.

'He shall be paid for these too,' said Aranrhod. 'But they are too small and will not go on me.'

The messengers reported this to Gwydion. 'I waste my craft,' he reproved them. 'I shall make no more shoes for her until I measure her foot myself.'

When she heard this, 'Yes,' said Aranrhod, 'that will be best. Tell him I am on my way.'

When she reached the ship Gwydion was cutting out and the boy stitching. 'Heaven prosper you, lady,' said Gwydion.

'Heaven prosper you too,' she replied. 'But I marvel that a man of your craft cannot make shoes to measure.'

'There is a reason for everything,' said Gwydion. 'I think I may succeed now.'

At that moment a wren alighted on board the ship. The boy took aim at it with his awl, so that he hit it between the sinew of its leg and the bone. Aranrhod laughed. 'Faith,' she said, 'with a deft hand has the fair one hit it.'

'Aye,' retorted Gwydion, 'he has hit more deftly than you know. For he has now got a name, and a very good name. Lleu Llaw Gyffes he shall be called from now on.' [Lleu: fair. Llaw: hand. Gyffes: deft.] And as he spoke the wren vanished into air, and the leathers into dulse, and where the ship had been there was only sea-girdle. Then he released his son into his proper semblance, and himself stood revealed in his right aspect. 'Lady,' he said, 'this is your son. It is not too late for you to make him amends.

'There is no hope of that,' she vowed. 'Moreover, I will swear on him a second destiny, that he shall never bear arms until he gets them from me.'

'Cruel woman,' cried Gwydion in his anger, 'to treat your own son thus! But never fear, he shall have arms, and sooner than you think.'

They returned now to Math's court, where Lleu Llaw Gyffes was reared till he could ride every horse and run every course, and till he was perfected in feature, form and favour, even as a man should be. But Gwydion saw that he was pining for want of arms, and at last he found a time to say to him: 'Lad, you and I will go a journey tomorrow. I know what you want, and we shall find it before we return. Till then, lad, be of good cheer.'

On the morrow in the young of the day they arose and followed the sea-shore towards Caer Aranrhod. When they were near enough to recognize the place, Gwydion changed their semblance, so that they came riding towards the land-gate of the castle in the guise of young men. Of the two, though,

Gwydion was the staider and stouter. 'Porter,' he ordered, 'go in and tell your lady that there are bards here from the south who would gladly entertain her.' The porter returned quickly and led them inside.

'A welcome to you both,' said Aranrhod, in answer to their greeting. They went to eat, and when that was ended there was much discourse of tales and storytelling, and all the court was happy that night, for Gwydion was the best teller of tales in the world.

Later a chamber was made ready for them and they went to sleep. At first cockcrow Gwydion arose by stealth and called up his magic and his power. By early dawn there was a bustling to and fro and trumpets and clamour throughout the countryside. By daylight they heard a knocking at the chamber door, and there was Aranrhod herself bidding them open. The boy arose and opened the door; she came in and a maiden with her.

'Good sirs,' she cried, 'we are in danger. You must rise and help defend the castle.'

'We have heard the trumpets and clamour,' Gwydion admitted. 'What is the cause of that, lady?'

'Faith,' she said, 'go to the embrasure and you will not know the colour of the sea for the host of ships you will spy there, making for the land with all the speed they can.'

'I see them, lady,' said Gwydion, 'and they are still more numerous than you say.'

'Then what shall we do? I beg you, good sirs, to find a plan for me.'

'There is only one plan I know,' Gwydion told her. 'We must close the castle gates and make the best defence we can.

Have you arms? Then bring them here and arm this youth and me.'

She went out after the arms and returned, and two maidens with her. 'Lady,' said Gwydion, 'do you arm this youth. I am staider and stouter, and the maidens will help me better than they would help him. Hurry, lady, hurry! Surely I hear men at the gates?'

In haste but with the properest care, Aranrhod armed the youth at all points. 'Is his arming completed?' asked Gwydion.

'At all points,' said Aranrhod. 'Now, acquit yourselves like men.'

Gwydion burst out laughing. 'It is time to doff our arms,' he corrected her, as she stood before him angry and puzzled.

'But why?' she demanded. 'Look at the fleet that surrounds us!'

'There is no fleet, lady.'

'Then hearken to the land army!'

'There is no army either.'

'Alas,' asked Aranrhod, 'what kind of a mustering was this?'

'A mustering,' he replied, 'to break the destiny you swore upon your son.' As he spoke these words he released his son into his proper semblance, and himself stood revealed in his right aspect. 'Here is your son, lady, who has received arms at your hands. Will you still not take him to you and love him as your own?'

'I am so far from doing that,' said the angry Aranrhod, 'that I will swear on him a third destiny, that he shall never have a wife of all the women that are now on earth.'

'Monstrous woman,' cried Gwydion, 'to treat your own

son thus! But never fear, lad,' he added more quietly, 'you shall have a wife, and sooner than she thinks.'

After they had broken their fast they left the castle, and without any halt made their way to the court of Math son of Mathonwy. The told him their troubles, and he commanded that his wand be put in his hand.

'Aye,' he told Gwydion, 'we shall be too much for her, you and I. Let us seek by our magic and enchantment to make a wife for him out of flowers.'

For Lleu was now a man in feature, form and favour, and the handsomest youth that mortal ever saw. They took the flowers of the oak, the broom, and the meadowsweet, and from those they called forth the fairest and the best endowed maiden that was ever seen in Gwynedd, and baptized her with the baptism they used at that time, and the name they gave her was Blodeuedd [Flowers]. Then they gave Lleu Llaw Gyffes a court and its territory, so that he might honourably maintain himself, in the place which is called Mur Castell in the uplands of Ardudwy, and he settled there and ruled it well, and every one was content with him and his rule.

A year passed, and a second, and then it happened one day that Lleu went to Caer Dathyl to visit Math and Gwydion. That same day, not long after he had gone, Blodeuedd was crossing the courtyard when she heard the blast of a horn, and after the blast she saw a spent stag going by, and after the stag there came dogs and huntsmen, and after these a troop of men on foot moving more slowly. She was curious to know who these men and their lord might be, and sent a lad to enquire. 'Gronw Bebyr is our lord here,' they told him; 'he who is lord of Penllyn.'

Meantime Gronw was pursuing the stag. The dogs pulled it down on the bank of Cynfael river, and it was there that he slew it. But what with killing the stag and feeding his dogs and the exhaustion of his horses, he was kept busy there till night closed in on him. Darkness was falling as he again came past the gate of the court.

'Faith,' said Blodeuedd, 'it would be a great discourtesy to let the chieftain pass by to some other dwelling at this hour of the night.' Messengers went out to meet Gronw and invite him to the court. He accepted the invitation gladly, and Blodeuedd herself came forth to meet him at the gate and gave him greeting.

'Lady,' he said, 'Heaven repay you this noble welcome.'

He washed and changed his hunting garb, and then they sat down. Blodeuedd looked on him where he sat, and as she looked she was filled with love of him, so that her cheeks were now red as the reddest foxgloves and now white as the foam of the sea. And Gronw looked on her, and the same thought was in him as in her, so that he might not conceal that he loved her; and from that same moment all their talk was of the love and affection they felt one for the other. And they talked too of how it might come about that they should be together for ever.

'There is only one plan I know,' Gronw told her. 'We must kill your husband Lleu.'

'Only one man in this world knows how his death may come about,' replied Blodeuedd. 'And Lleu is that man.'

'Then under pretence of loving care for him,' said Gronw, 'you must win his secret from him.' And before he rode away from the court he said again: 'Remember, lady, what I told you. For you alone can draw from him what way his death may come about.'

The first thing Lleu noticed when he reached home was that his wife was sad and silent. 'Lady,' he asked her, 'are you ill or does some trouble oppress you? I cannot bear to see you unhappy.'

'I am not ill,' she replied, 'but I am troubled about you in a way you would never trouble about me. I am troubled about your death, lest you should die sooner than I.'

'Ah,' said Lleu, 'Heaven repay you for your loving care. But be happy, for unless God shall slay me, I shall not easily be slain.'

'I thank Heaven for it,' replied his wife. 'But tell me how that may be, for my memory should prove a surer safeguard than yours.'

'I will, gladly,' said Lleu. 'First, it will not be easy to kill me with a blow. The spear that would kill me must be a whole year a-making, and never a hand shall be laid to that work except when other folk are at Mass on Sunday.'

'I thank Heaven for it,' replied his wife.

'Further, I cannot be slain inside or outside a house. I cannot be slain on horseback or a-foot.'

'Why,' she said, 'then you cannot be slain at all.'

'Yes,' he told her, 'I can be slain by this means. By making a bath for me on a river bank, and setting a vaulted frame over the tub, and thatching it well and snugly, and then bringing a he-goat and placing it alongside the tub, and then I myself setting one foot on the back of the goat and the other on the edge of the tub. If anyone should smite me with a one-year spear when I was standing so, he would bring about my death.'

'I thank Heaven for it,' replied his wife. 'For that can be easily avoided.'

She had news of this sent to Gronw in Penllyn, and for a whole year Gronw laboured to make the spear, and that same day twelvemonth he had her informed that it was ready.

'Lord,' she said to Lleu, 'I am still troubled about the manner of your death. That is a thing I would guard against more than my own death or the kingdom's. Will you show me in what manner you would stand on the back of the goat and the edge of the tub, if I prepare the bath?'

'Heaven repay you for your loving care,' replied Lleu. 'I will show you gladly.'

This news too she had sent to Gronw, with an instruction that he should be lying in wait under the lee of a hill on the bank of Cynfael river. Also she had all the he-goats of the district gathered together on the bank facing that hill. Then on the morrow she said to Lleu, 'Lord, I have had the bath and the frame prepared, and they are ready for you. Will you look?' So they came to look at the bath. 'Will you go into the bath, as you promised, lord?' she asked. He went into the bath. 'And here are the animals you called he-goats,' she told him. 'Shall one of them be fetched here alongside the bath?' A goat was fetched, and Lleu rose up out of the bath and stood with one foot on the back of the goat and the other on the edge of the tub. At that moment Gronw drew himself up on one knee from behind the lee of the hill and took aim at him with the poisoned spear, and smote him in the side, so that the shaft started out of him and the head remained embedded. Instantly he flew up in the form of an eagle and gave a horrid scream. And after that he was seen no more.

The moment he vanished Gronw and Blodeuedd set off for the court, and the next day Gronw rose up and subdued Ardudwy, so that all Lleu's lands were under his sway.

News of these events was brought to Math son of Mathonwy and to Gwydion son of Dôn. Their grief grew heavy upon them. 'Lord king,' said Gwydion, 'I shall never rest till I get tidings of my son. Give me leave that I may make the circuit of Gwynedd.'

'Aye,' said Math, 'may God be your guide.' Gwydion set off that same day and traversed Gwynedd and the length and breadth of Powys, but he found no word or whisper of his son Lleu. In time he arrived at the house of a villein in Arfon and took lodging for the night. The goodman came home late, and last of all came the swineherd.

'Fellow,' asked the goodman, 'has your sow come home tonight?'

'Aye,' he replied. 'She has just gone into the sty.'

'What kind of journey does that sow go on?' asked Gwydion.

'That is what no one knows,' was the answer. 'Every day when the sty is opened she goes off at such a run that no one has as yet been able to keep up with her. For all I know,' said the swineherd, 'she might as well disappear into the depths of the earth.'

'Do me one favour,' asked Gwydion. 'Do not open the sty until I am standing there at your side.'

'Gladly,' said the swineherd, and they named a time of day for tomorrow's morn.

When the swineherd saw the first light of day he roused Gwydion, and they went and stood alongside the sty. The moment the sty was opened out rushed the sow and made upstream at top speed into the valley which is now called Nantlleu, where she slowed down and began to feed under an oak. Gwydion had followed her, and came forward under the tree to see what she was feeding on. Her food, he could see, was rotten flesh and maggots. So he looked up into the tree, and in the tree top he could see an eagle. And whenever the eagle shook himself the worms and the rotten flesh fell from him. Gwydion thought that this eagle must be Lleu, and he sang a verse:

> *'Grows an oak within this glen*
> *'Twixt two lakes (the dark sky lours);*
> *If I speak not falsely, then*
> *This befalls from Lleu's false flower.'*

When he heard Gwydion's voice the eagle descended till he was in the middle of the tree. Then Gwydion sang a second verse:

> *'Grows an oak on upland plain,*
> *Heat and tempest pass it by;*
> *Of nine-score hardships he'll complain,*
> *In its top, the deft-hand Lleu.'*

The eagle now let himself down till he was on the lowest branch of the tree. Then Gwydion sang yet a third verse:

> *'Grows an oak upon a hill,*
> *Fair lord's refuge this, maybe;*
> *If I speak not falsely, still*
> *Lleu will light upon my knee.'*

At these words the eagle came down and alighted on Gwydion's knee. Then Gwydion struck him with his magic wand, so that he was once more in his own likeness. No one ever saw on man a more pitiful sight. He was nothing but skin and bone.

With great tenderness Gwydion conveyed him to Caer Dathyl, to Math's court, and all the physicians of Gwynedd came there to heal him. But it was a full year before he was whole again. As soon as he was whole he came to speak to Math. 'Lord king,' he said, 'it is time for me to get redress from the man who brought this suffering upon me. And the sooner I get it, the better satisfied I shall be.'

Math mustered Gwynedd, and Lleu and his father set out for Ardudwy. Gwydion travelled in front and was soon in sight of Mur Castell. Blodeuedd was informed that they were coming, and such was her fear that she fled across the river with her maidens and far out on to the mountain. Here all her maidens fell into a deep lake and were drowned, and she was alone when Gwydion caught up with her.

'Do not kill me,' she begged. 'I am young. Why should I die?'

'No,' he said , 'I will not kill you.' At his words she laughed and cried together, but he would not pity her even so. 'There is a harder destiny for you by far than to die. I shall release you in the shape of a bird, and because of the dishonour you have done to my son Lleu, you shall never dare show your face by daylight, through fear of other birds, so that it will be their nature to mob and molest you wherever they find you. Nor shall you lose your name Blodeuedd [Flowers], but I will change it a little even so, so that now and for ever you shall be called Blodeuwedd [Flowerface].'

And that is the reason why all birds are hostile to the owl, and why the owl is called Blodeuwedd to this present day.

Meantime Gronw Bebyr had fled to Penllyn, whence he sent envoys to ask whether Lleu Llaw Gyffes would accept land or territory or gold or silver for his injury. 'Not I,' vowed Lleu. 'The very least I will accept of him is that he shall stand in the place where I stood, and I in the place where he stood, and that I shall then take aim at him with my spear.'

This answer was brought to Gronw. 'Aye,' he said, 'that is the least I can do. My trusty lords, my war-band, and my foster-brothers, is there any one of you will take this blow in my stead?'

'Faith,' they answered, 'there is none.' And that is why they have been called from that day to this one of the Three Disloyal War-bands.

'Then if that is so,' said Gronw, 'I must needs take it myself.'

The two of them came to the bank of Cynfael river. Then Gronw stood in the place where Lleu had been when he smote him with the spear, and Lleu in the lee of the hill.

'Lord,' said Gronw then, 'since it was through a woman's wiles I did you so much hurt, I beg you for pity's sake that you will let me set that great stone I see there between me and the blow.'

'I will not refuse you that,' said Lleu.

So Gronw took up the stone and set it between him and the blow. Then Lleu rose up on one knee and took aim at him with the spear, and the spear pierced the stone and Gronw too, so that his back was broken and that was the end of him. The stone may be seen there to this day, on the bank of

Cynfael river, and the hole goes right through it. And for that reason it is called Llech Ronw [Gronw's Stone].

And when he had slain Gronw, Lleu Llaw Gyffes took possession of the land a second time and ruled over it prosperously. And in the fullness of time, so the tale tells, he succeeded Math as king over Gwynedd. And that is the end of his story.

THE
BRITISH
ARTHUR

❖

THE QUEST FOR OLWEN
I
The Destiny

——— ❖ ———

It was the wish of King Cilydd, a mighty one of this Island, that he might have a wife as well born as himself. So he married the princess Goleuddydd, and it was at once the wish and hope of the whole countryside that they might have children, and more especially a son. But Goleuddydd became mad and ran away to the wilds, and it was there, near a place where a swineherd was keeping a herd of swine, that she gave birth to a lovely boy. The swineherd took the boy and his mother to the King's court, and they gave him the name Culhwch. He was first cousin to Arthur. The boy was then put out to nurse.

Soon afterwards his mother Goleuddydd grew sick and feared that she would die. She had her husband called to her, and, 'I am going to die of this sickness, husband,' she told him, 'and then you will wish for another wife. It will be for her, I know, to dispense your gifts, but remember, it would be wicked of you to rob our only son of his due. Will you promise me one thing before I die?'

'Gladly,' said King Cilydd. 'Name your request.'

'I ask you not to take a wife again till you shall see a two-headed briar growing on my grave. Will you promise?'

'I promise,' he said. 'But not gladly.'

'Gladly or not,' she assured him, 'I can now die at peace.'

She sent for her preceptor and bade him clean the grave so thoroughly each year that not the tiniest herb or plant or flower might grow on it. And then she died.

For seven years the preceptor kept his word: the grave stayed bare. Every morning the King would send an attendant to see whether anything was growing there yet, but he had always the same answer: nothing. Then the preceptor grew old and lazy, and at last he neglected his task altogether, and that was how it happened that one day, when the King rode home from hunting past the graveyard, he looked inside and saw something growing there. When he looked closer it was a briar, and when he looked closest of all it was a briar with two heads.

'It is time now for me to take a wife again,' he told his counsellors. 'Whom do you think I should take?'

'I know of a lady who would suit you in every way,' one of them replied. 'She is the wife of King Doged.'

They decided to go and find her. First they slew the king her husband, and then they brought her home with them, and her only child, a daughter, along with her. In no time at all she was Cilydd's queen and the dispenser of his gifts. But, strangely enough, no one saw fit to tell her of Culhwch's existence.

One day when she was out walking she came to the house of an old crone who was living nearby. She went inside, and there was the crone, without a tooth in her head, sitting over the fire. 'Tell me, crone,' she said, 'for no one else seems willing to: where are the children of the man who has carried me off by force?'

'Why,' answered the crone, 'he has no children.'

'Unhappy lady that I am,' cried the Queen, 'to be given to a childless man!'

She looked so miserable at this news that the crone took pity on her, and, beckoning her closer, she whispered in her ear: 'Be less unhappy, lady, for he has one son, the prince Culhwch.'

'Crone,' said the Queen, 'name your reward.' Then she hurried back home to speak to the king her husband. 'Why should you hide your son, the prince Culhwch, from me?' she asked indignantly.

'At least,' replied the King, 'I will hide him no longer.'

Messengers were sent after the boy that very day, and he returned to the court. 'What a handsome lad I have for a stepson,' said the Queen. 'You look to me of an age to take a wife, lad.' Here she beckoned to her daughter. 'And it so happens that I have a daughter of my own who would make a wife fit for any prince in the world.'

'I am too young to take a wife,' said the boy, shaking his head. 'I am afraid I cannot marry your daughter.'

This put the Queen in a high rage. 'If you will not marry my daughter,' she threatened, 'I will swear a destiny upon you, that you shall never have a wife in all your days until you win for your bride Olwen, the daughter of Ysbaddaden Chief Giant.'

At these words, though he had never even heard of Olwen, the boy was filled with such love of her, and his colour changed so fast, that his father asked, 'Son, son, what troubles you? Why do you change from red to white, and white to red, so fast?'

'Because of the destiny sworn upon me by my step-mother,' he replied, 'that I shall never have a wife till I win the maid Olwen. Do you know where I can find her, father?'

'Alas, son,' he said, 'if I knew, I would tell you, but I have heard neither word nor whisper of that maiden. But take heart,' he told him. 'Arthur is your first cousin. Go to his court and get him to trim your hair, and then he must promise you whatever gift you request of him. In the name of his warriors and the gold-torqued maidens of this Island you will then ask him for Olwen.'

'If I can do no more, I can likewise do no less,' said the boy. 'If I can go late, I can as well go soon.'

And when he had embraced his father, and given him the greeting proper for a king, he left the hall and prepared for his journey to the court of his kinsman Arthur.

At Arthur's Court

———— ❖ ————

Off rode the boy on a steed with light-grey head, four winters old, shell-hoofed, with well-knit fork, and with a gold bridle-bit in its mouth. Under him was a precious gold saddle, and in his hand he bore two whetted spears of silver. He bore a battle-axe too, the forearm's length of a full-grown man from ridge to edge; it would draw blood from the wind, and was swifter than the swiftest dew-drop from the stalk to the ground, when the dew-fall is heaviest in the month of June. On his thigh he carried a gold-hilted sword, its blade golden too; and slung about him was a gold-chased buckler with an ivory boss. Two greyhounds ran before him, brindled and white-breasted, with a collar of red gold about the neck of either from shoulder-swell to ear; the one on his left side would be on the right, and the one on his right side would be on the left, so that they were like two sea-mews sporting around him. The four clods the four hooves of his steed would cut were like four swallows in the air over his head, now before him, now behind. He had a four-cornered mantle of purple silk upon him, with an apple of red gold in each of its corners, and each apple worth a hundred kine; while his foot-gear and stirrups, from the top of his thigh to the tip of his toe, were worth three hundred kine in purest gold. And not a hair-tip stirred upon his head, so lightly did his steed canter under him on his way to the gate of Arthur's court.

'Is there a porter?' he demanded, when he reached the gate.

'There is,' was the answer. 'And a curse on your head that you ask!'

'And who are you,' asked the boy, 'that I may the better resent your rudeness?'

'I am Arthur's porter each first day of January. But for the rest of the year I have as my deputies Huandaw and Gogigwr and Llaesgymin the Slack-hewer, and best of all Penpingion, who goes on his head to spare his feet, neither heavenwards nor earthwards, but like a rolling stone on a court floor.'

'Then if you are Arthur's porter, open Arthur's gate.'

'I will not,' said the rude porter.

'Why will you not open it?'

'Because knife has gone into meat, and drink into horn, and there is a thronging in Arthur's hall. Save for the son of a king of a rightful dominion, or a craftsman who brings his craft, no one may enter. But in the hospice yonder there is meat for your dogs and corn for your horse, and hot peppered chops for yourself, and wine brimming over, and delectable songs before you. Tomorrow at the third hour, when the gate is opened for today's host, you may enter and sit where you will in Arthur's hall.'

'I will have none of that,' answered the boy. 'Open the gate and all shall be well; but if not, I will bring dishonour upon Arthur and ill fame upon you, his porter. I will raise three shouts at this gate which shall be so shrill and dreadful that all the world will miscarry for the noise.'

'Bawl your head off, if you want to,' retorted Glewlwyd Mighty-grasp the porter, 'but you shall not pass through my gate till I have first spoken with Arthur.'

Glewlwyd went into the hall.

Said Arthur: 'You have news from the gate?'

'I have, lord. Two-thirds of my life are past, and two-thirds of your own, and always we have been together, in raids and hunts and slaughters. And I shall be with you till the end, whatever that end may be. I tell you now, king: fair lordly men we have seen, men handsome as the stars in heaven, but I never saw a man as handsome as he that is now at the gate.'

'Then bring him in,' said Arthur. 'Let some serve him with gold drinking-horns, and others with hot peppered chops. It is a shameful thing to leave in wind and rain so fine a man as you tell of. Is that not so, Cei?'

'By the hand of my friend,' answered the blunt Cei, 'if you ask my advice, I should not alter the customs of court for his sake.'

'Not so, Cei,' Arthur reproved him. 'We are the nobler in that such fine men resort to us. And the greater our bounty proves, the greater shall be our fame.'

So Glewlwyd opened the gate, and Culhwch, without dismounting at the horse-block outside, rode on his steed with a clatter into the hall, and drew rein before Arthur's throne.

'Hail, sovereign prince of this Island!' he cried. 'My greetings to you.'

'My greetings to you too,' said Arthur. 'You shall have food and song here with me tonight, and in the morning, when I dispense gifts, I shall begin at your hand.'

'I am not here,' said the boy proudly, 'to wheedle food and drink. I am here to ask a boon.'

'Name it,' replied Arthur, 'and you shall obtain it, as far as wind dries and rain wets, sun runs and sea stretches, as far as earth itself extends, save only that I may grant it with honour.'

'I would have my hair trimmed,' said Culhwch.

'And so you shall,' promised Arthur. 'My heart grows tender towards you. I am sure you are a kinsman of mine.' Taking up a golden comb and shears with loops of silver, he trimmed his yellow hair. 'And now,' he ordered, 'tell me who you are.' And when he had heard, 'Why,' he said, 'you are my first cousin. Name any gift you will, and you shall have it gladly.'

Said Culhwch: 'I would have Olwen daughter of Ysbaddaden Chief Giant for my wife; and there is a destiny upon me that I shall have no other. That is why I ask for her here in your court, in the name of all these warriors, and in the name too of the gentle gold-torqued maidens of the Island of Britain.'

He asked for his gift in the name of Gwyn son of Nudd, and Cilydd Hundred-holds, and Canhastyr Hundred-hands, and Cors Hundred-claws, and Taliesin Chief of Bards (one of the seven men who came alive from Ireland after the death of his lord Brân), and Morfran son of Tegid (no man placed his weapon in him at the battle of Camlan, so very ugly was he; all thought he was a devil helping), and Sandde Angel-face (no man placed his spear in him at Camlan, so very fair was he; all thought he was an angel helping), and Sgilti Lightfoot (when the whim to run his lord's errand was in him, he never needed a road; wherever there was forest, along the tree-tops he would go, and where there was a moor, along the tips of the reeds; and in all his life never a reed bent beneath his feet, much less did one break, so very light of foot was he), and Drem the Seer (who saw from Cornwall to Pictland when a fly would rise up in the morning with the sun), and Clust the Hearer (if he were buried seven fathom deep in the earth, he would hear an ant fifty miles off when it stirred from its couch in the morning), and Ôl the Tracker (whose father's pigs were carried off seven years before he was born, and who, when he grew to man's estate, tracked the pigs, and brought them home in seven herds), and Paris king of France (from whom the city of Paris gets its name), and Eli and Trachmyr, Arthur's head huntsmen, and Gilla Stag-shank, the chief leaper of Ireland, and Huarwar the Hungry (he was one of the three great plagues of Cornwall and Devon till his fill was found him; no glimmer of a smile was ever seen on him till he was sated), and Sugyn the Thirsty (who would suck up the sea on which there were three hundred ships till all that remained was a dry strand), and Bwlch and Cyfwlch and Syfwlch (three gleaming glitterers their three shields; three pointed piercers their three spears; three keen carvers their three swords), and Cei and Bedwyr and Gwalchmei (whom the English call Gawain)—in the name of these and armies of others Culhwch asked for his gift.

And he asked for it further, in the name of the gentle gold-torqued maidens of this Island (in addition to Gwenhwyfar, the white-phantom queen, and Gwenhwyach her fairer sister): Celemon daughter of Cei, and Gwen the White-swan, daughter of Cynwal Hundred-hogs; fair Gwenlliant the magnanimous maiden, and Creiddylad daughter of Lludd Silver-hand (the maiden of most majesty that was ever in the Island of Britain and its three adjacent islands), and Esyllt Whiteneck, and Esyllt Slenderneck—in the name of these too, and of many others, he asked for Arthur's gift.

'Chieftain,' said Arthur, 'I have heard neither word nor whisper of the maid Olwen, nor of her parents. Yet I will gladly send messengers to seek her.'

Widely these messengers journeyed till the end of a year, but when they reached Arthur's court again, they were no wiser than the day they set out. 'We do not know, lord,' they told Arthur, 'nor can we believe, that there is any such maiden to be found in the world.'

'Chieftain,' said Arthur, 'you hear my men?'

'I do not choose to hear,' retorted Culhwch. 'All other men have what they asked for here, and I stand empty-handed. If I leave your court without her, lord, I must bear your honour and your broken promise with me.'

But Cei spoke from where he sat at Arthur's right hand. 'You do wrong, chieftain,' he said, 'to blame Arthur. But come to seek her with me and my comrades, and till the day you declare that she does not exist in the world, or till we find her, we shall never be parted from you.'

Then Arthur arose. First he called on Cei for this enterprise. It was of Cei that his father said these words: 'If there is anything of me in him, his heart will be a cold one. And it will be his way to be headstrong ever.' Cei had this peculiarity, that his breath lasted nine nights and nine days under water, and that nine nights and nine days he might go without sleep. Also, a wound from Cei's sword might never be healed by any physician. When he wished, he could be as tall as the tallest tree in the forest; and when the rain was at its heaviest, whatever lay in his hand would keep dry, by reason of his own great heat. On enterprises he was Arthur's best servant; in battles he was his first fighter.

Second, Arthur called on Bedwyr, who never shrank from an enterprise upon which Cei was bound. Only Arthur and one other in Britain were as handsome as Bedwyr, and he had this peculiarity, that though he had only one hand, no three warriors drew blood on the battlefield faster than he. His spear had this quality, that when he had thrust with it once, it made nine more thrusts of its own.

Third, Arthur called on Cynddylig the Guide. 'Go, friend,' he said, 'on this enterprise for me.' He was as good a guide in a land he had never seen as in his own country.

Fourth, he called on Gwrhyr Interpreter of Tongues. He knew all tongues of men and beasts and birds, and fishes too.

Fifth, he called on Gwalchmei, his nephew, because he never returned home without what he had gone to seek. He was the best marcher and the best rider among Arthur's men.

Last he called on Menw, so that if they came among heathens or monsters he might cast a spell over them, and though none should see them, yet they might see every one.

And so it was that when they had equipped themselves with horses, food, and weapons, and with Arthur's blessing and the grumbles of the porter like bells on their ears, Culhwch and the Helping Companions set out on their hard quest.

III

In Search of Olwen

❖

For a long time these men were wandering the bounds and the wastes of this Island, till one day they reached a wide open plain, where they saw a fort which was the biggest in the world. They travelled the whole day, but so wide was the plain that they thought themselves no nearer to the fort than before. The second day it was the same, but on the third they came near enough to see by the fort a huge flock of sheep, without end or limit to it, and a shepherd in a jerkin of skins watching the sheep from the top of a green mound. But it was the mastiff at his side which drew their attention most. He was bigger than a nine-year-old stallion, and so savage that none might escape his jaws and deadly injury. His very breath was so fearsome that it had burned all the nearby trees and bushes to the ground; and yet, so clever was he, that he and the shepherd had never lost a lamb, much less a grown beast, that was given into their charge.

'Gwrhyr,' said Cei. 'You are our interpreter. Go and have word with the shepherd yonder.'

'Cei,' replied Gwrhyr, 'my pledge was to go only as far as you yourself go.'

'Very well,' said Cei. 'Then let us go forward together.'

'Do not be afraid—' began Menw.

'Afraid!' cried Cei.

'For I will cast a spell over the dog, so that he can neither see us nor harm us.'

'If you think it necessary, do so,' was Cei's scornful answer; but in his heart he was glad enough to trick the dog in this way.

In an hour or so they reached the shepherd on his mound, and gave him greeting. He was rather short with them in reply.

'Things are well with you, shepherd,' said Cei, indicating the immense flock that surrounded the mound.

'May they never be better with you than with me,' he answered, and left them to make what they could of his words.

'Whose sheep might these be?' asked Gwalchmei the bold.

'Fools of men that you are! Every one in the world knows that these are the sheep of Ysbaddaden Chief Giant, and that this is his fort.'

'That is what we were thinking,' said Gwalchmei quickly. 'And you, friend, who are you?'

'I am the shepherd Custennin, and you see me in this guise because Ysbaddaden Chief Giant has wrought my ruin. But what men are you,' he asked, 'that my dog has not scented and mangled you?'

'We are messengers of Arthur,' announced Cei, 'and we are here to seek Olwen, the Giant's daughter.'

'Whew!' said the shepherd—and the dog bounded high at his whistle. 'Try anything, friends, but that!'

'And what,' demanded Culhwch, 'is wrong with our seeking the maid Olwen?'

'Alas, young man, I have seen many come on this same

quest, but I have not seen one depart with his life, much less with Olwen. But surely,' said the shepherd, looking closer, 'you are Culhwch son of Cilydd and Goleuddydd his first queen? My heart grows tender towards you, for you are my nephew, my wife's sister's son.' He came down from the mound to embrace him. 'You must come to see my wife, who will help you, though I must warn you that she is the strongest woman in the world, so that it is as well to meet her warily.'

'There is no woman alive that I am afraid of,' replied Cei. 'Shepherd, lead the way.'

'Well, we shall soon see,' remarked Custennin; and with a word to the dog to stay on guard over the giant's flock, he escorted them to the gate of his ruined court.

When his wife heard the noise of their coming, she came running joyously to meet them. 'My heart grows tender within me,' she cried. 'There is someone here both near and dear to me.'

'That is he,' said her husband, pointing at Cei, and she rushed towards him, to try and throw her thick strong arms about his neck. But Cei was quick enough to fling a big log off the wood-pile into her hands, and it was as well that he did so, for the very next moment the log lay crushed and splintered on the ground. 'Woman,' said Cei, 'had it been I that you squeezed in this manner, there would be no need for another to love me now or for ever.' And he shook his head between mirth and dismay.

'There is a lesson in everything,' said the shepherd, and they went on inside the house where their needs were supplied. Then, as soon as she knew that they were friends, his wife opened a big stone coffer which stood by the hearth, and there came climbing out of it a handsome lad with curly yellow hair. 'He is the only one left to me,' she lamented. 'Ysbaddaden Chief Giant has slain the other twenty-three of my sons, and I have no better hope of keeping this one than the rest.'

'Let him join company with me,' promised Cei; and all the Helping Companions cried 'Aye!' 'And if he is slain thereafter, it will be because I have been slain first.'

For a time they ate and drank, and then, 'What is your errand here, friends?' the woman asked them. 'Is it one where I can help?'

'We are here to seek Olwen daughter of Ysbaddaden Chief Giant.'

'Whew!' she whistled, just like her husband. 'Since no one from the fort has seen you, flee at once to Arthur's court. Otherwise you must all lose your lives.'

'We will not flee until we see Olwen,' vowed Cei.

'Nor then either,' said Culhwch. 'Does she ever come to this court?'

'Every Saturday she comes here to wash her hair; and in the bowl where she washes she leaves her rings, and they are all of pure gold.'

'Will she come now if she is sent for?'

The shepherd's wife nodded. 'If you pledge your word that you will do her no harm, I will send for her.'

'We pledge it,' they said.

So she was sent for. And she came, with a robe of flame-red silk about her, and around the maiden's neck a collar of red gold, and precious pearls thereon and rubies. Yellower was her hair than the flower of the broom, whiter was her flesh than the foam of the wave; and whiter her palms and her fingers than the shoots of the marsh trefoil from amidst the fine gravel of a welling spring. Neither the eye of the mewed hawk, nor the eye of the thrice-mewed falcon, nor any eye in the whole wide world was fairer than hers. Her breast was whiter than the breast of the white swan; and her cheeks were redder than the reddest foxgloves. All who beheld her would be filled with love of her. Four white trefoils sprang up behind her wherever she walked; and for that reason she was called Olwen [Whitetrack].

She entered the house and sat between Culhwch and the high seat, and even as he saw her he knew her. 'Ah, maiden,' he said, 'it is you I have loved. Come now with me.'

But she shook her head. 'That would be ill done of us both,' she told him. 'My father has taken a pledge of me that I will never leave him without his consent, for he knows that he shall live only until my husband takes me, and then he must die. No, what you must do is this. Go and ask me at my father's hand, and whatever tasks he may demand of you, those you must promise to perform. Win for him all he asks, and you shall win me too. But otherwise you shall hardly escape with your lives.'

They promised to do this, and she left them. Then they arose to go after her to the fort, and slew nine gatemen who were at nine gates without a man crying out, and nine mastiffs without one squealing. They went forward to the hall and greeted Ysbaddaden Chief Giant.

'And you,' he shouted, 'where do you think you are going?'

'We are going to seek Olwen your daughter for Culhwch son of Cilydd.'

'I cannot see you,' he roared. 'Where are those ruffians of

servants of mine?' And when they ran humbly in, 'Prop the forks under my two eyelids,' he ordered, 'so that I may see my future son-in-law.' This was done. Forks like trees were set to raise his eyelids from his eyes. 'Come back tomorrow,' he told them. 'I shall have an answer for you then.'

They turned to go, and the moment their backs were turned Ysbaddaden Chief Giant snatched at one of the three poisoned stone-spears which lay to his hand and hurled it after them. But Bedwyr caught it in his one hand and hurled it back at him, and it pierced Ysbaddaden right through the ball of his knee. 'Oh, oh, oh!' he bellowed. 'You cursed savage son-in-law! I shall walk the worse up a slope for this. Like the sting of a gadfly the poisoned iron has pained me. Cursed be the smith who fashioned it, and the anvil on which it was wrought!'

That night they lodged in Custennin's house, but on the morrow with pomp and ceremony, and with brave combs set in their hair, they entered the Giant's hall.

'Chief Giant,' they said, 'give us your daughter in return for her portion and a dowry to you and her two kinswomen. Only harm and death can be your lot otherwise.'

'No,' he shouted. 'Her four great-grandmothers and her four great-grandfathers are still alive. I can do nothing till I take counsel with them. Come back tomorrow. I shall have an answer for you then.'

They turned to go, and this time Ysbaddaden Chief Giant snatched at the second of the three poisoned stone-spears which lay to his hand and hurled it after them. But Menw caught it in full flight and hurled it back at him, and it pierced him through the middle of his breast, so that it came out at the small of his back. 'Oh, oh, oh!' he bellowed. 'You cursed savage son-in-law! I shall have pains in my chest and pains in my back for this, and how I shall eat food I simply don't know. Like the bite of a big-headed leech the hard iron has pained me. Cursed be the forge wherein it was heated!'

The third day again they came to court. 'Shoot at us no more, Chief Giant,' they warned him. 'Only harm and deadly hurt and death can be your lot if you do.'

'Where are my servants?' he shouted. 'Prop up the forks—my eyelids have fallen over the balls of my eyes—so that I can take a look at my future son-in-law. Come back tomorrow. I shall have an answer for you then.'

They turned to go, and now Ysbaddaden Chief Giant snatched at the third poisoned stone-spear and hurled it after them. But Culhwch caught it in full flight and hurled it back at him, and it pierced through the ball of the eye, so that it came out at the nape of his neck. 'Oh, oh, oh!' he bellowed. 'You cursed savage son-in-law! The sight of my eyes will be none the better for this. When I walk into the wind they will water, I shall have headaches a-plenty, and a giddiness with each new moon. Like the bite of a mad dog the poisoned iron has pained me. Cursed be the smith, and the anvil, and the forge, and all to do with its making!'

The fourth day again they came to court. 'Shoot at us no more, Chief Giant,' they urged him. 'Only harm and deadly hurt and martyrdom can be your lot if you do. Come now, give us your daughter.'

'Where is the man that seeks her? Step forward where I can see you. Prop up my eyelids, you scoundrels of servants! Oh, it is you, is it?'

'None other than I, Culhwch son of Cilydd.'

'Then you must promise me to do what is just,' cried the Giant.

'I promise.'

'It is easy to promise,' said the Giant, 'but only when I have obtained all that I shall name to you, shall you win my daughter.'

'Name it,' said Culhwch. 'And you shall have it all.'

'You see the big thicket yonder?' said Ysbaddaden. 'I must have it uprooted and burnt, and the land ploughed and sown, to make bread for your wedding guests and my daughter's, and all that must be done in one day.'

'It is easy for me to do that,' promised Culhwch, 'though you think it is not easy.'

'Though you get that, there is that you will not get. The horn of Gawlgawd to pour out for us at the wedding, and the cup of Llwyr son of Llwyrion, in which is the best of all drink. They will not give these vessels of their own free will, nor can you compel them.'

'It is easy for me to get that, though you think it is not easy.'

'Though you get that, there is that you will not get. The hamper of Gwyddno Long-shank, who ruled the Drowned Kingdom: if the whole world should come around it, thrice nine men at a time, all would find in it just such food as they desire. I must eat from that hamper upon the day of your wedding. He will not give it of his own free will, nor can you compel him.'

'It is easy for me to get that, though you think it is not easy.'

'Though you get that, there is that you will not get. The birds of Rhiannon, that wake the dead and lull the living to sleep, I must have to entertain me that night.'

'It is easy for me to get that, though you think it is not easy.'

'Though you get that, there is that you will not get. When first I met the mother of that maiden, I sowed nine hestors of flax seed in the hoed plot you see younder, but what became of it no man knows. I must have that seed back in the ground, so that it sprouts and grows, so that a white veil may be made from it for my daughter's head on the day of the wedding.'

'It is easy for me to get that, though you think it is not easy.'

'Then I must wash my head and shave my beard. I must have the tusk of Ysgithyrwyn Chief Boar with which to shave myself. Nor will I entrust the safe-keeping of the tusk to any save Cadw of Pictland, who will not leave his kingdom for any man, nor can you compel him. Besides, I must dress my beard before it is shaved, and nothing will do for that save the blood of the Black Witch, daughter of the White Witch, from the head of the Valley of Grief in the uplands of Hell.

'Further, there is no comb and shears in the world with which my hair may be dressed (see how stiff it is!) save the comb and shears that lie between the two ears of the boar Twrch Trwyth. Twrch Trwyth cannot be hunted till you obtain the whelp Drudwyn; and no leash will hold Drudwyn save the leash of Cors Hundred-claws. No collar will hold that leash save the collar of Canhastyr Hundred-hands, and only the chain of Cilydd Hundred-holds can hold both the collar and the leash.

'Further, there is no huntsman in the world can act as groom to that whelp save Mabon son of Modron, who was stolen away when he was three nights old from betwixt his mother and the wall. Where he is now is unknown, or what his state is, whether dead or alive. Nor will it ever be known unless his kinsman Eidoel is found first, and Eidoel is in Glini's secret prison, no one in the world knows where. And even Mabon cannot hunt Twrch Trwyth save on Gwyn Dun-mane (swift as a wave is he!) the steed of Gweddw, who will not give him of his own free will, nor can you compel him.

'Further, Twrch Trwyth cannot be hunted until the dogs Aned and Aethlem are obtained, who are swift as the wind and were never unleashed on the beast they did not kill. There is no huntsman in the world can hold those two dogs save Cyledyr the Wild son of Hetwn the Leper, and he is nine times wilder than the wildest beast on the mountain. Nor shall you obtain Cyledyr till first you obtain Gwyn son of Nudd, under whom God has set the demons of the Otherworld, lest this world should be destroyed by them. Of all men, he will never be spared from his charge.

'Further, no leash in the world will hold those two dogs unless it is made from the beard of Dillus the Bearded. Even that will be useless unless it is plucked from his beard while he is yet alive, and twitched forth with wooden tweezers. He will not allow anyone to do that to him while he lives, but it will be useless if he is dead, for then it will be brittle.

'Further, Twrch Trwyth cannot be hunted until Bwlch and Cyfwlch and Syfwlch are obtained. Three gleaming glitterers their three shields; three pointed piercers their three spears; three keen carvers their three swords. And these three men shall wind their horns with so dreadful a note that no one would care though the sky should tumble to earth.

'Further, Twrch Trwyth cannot be slain save with the sword of Wrnach the Giant. He will not give that sword for price nor favour, nor can you compel him.

'Last, Twrch Trwyth cannot be hunted without Arthur and his huntsmen. He is a man of might and lord of a true dom111on, and he will not come to help you. Speak now, son-in-law! Does your promise still stand?'

'Horses I shall have and horsemen to ride them,' answered Culhwch, 'and my kinsman Arthur will get me all those things you name. And I shall win your daughter, and you will lose your life.'

'If Arthur is your kinsman, a curse on him and you! Set forward now, with wakefulness and care, and when these things are won, you shall win my daughter too.'

And after these words Ysbaddaden Chief Giant knocked away the forks from under his eyelids, to show that their talk was over, and Culhwch and his friends went out of his presence with one eye looking over their shoulder.

IV

Fulfilling the Tasks

———— ❖ ————

(i) *The sword of Wrnach the Giant*

So once again Culhwch and the Helping Companions set forth on their travels. They journeyed all day till the evening, and then saw before them a great fortress of mortared stone, the biggest in the world. And coming from it they saw a black man, who was bigger than any three of mortal men.

'Whose fort is this?' they asked him, but he was short with them in reply. 'Fools of men that you are! Everyone knows that this is the fort of Wrnach the Giant.'

'News indeed,' said the blunt Cei. 'And what treatment is there for a guest and far-comer who alights at the fort?'

'I tell you, friend,' said the black man, 'that no guest has ever come away from it with his life. Besides, save for a craftsman who brings his craft, no one may enter there.'

They pressed on their way to the gate. 'Is there a porter?' demanded Cei.

'There is,' was the answer, 'and a curse on your head that you ask!'

'Then if you are Wrnach's porter, open Wrnach's gate.'

'I will not,' said the rude porter.

'Why will you not open it?'

'Because knife has gone into meat, and drink into horn, and there is a thronging in Wrnach's hall. Save for a craftsman who brings his craft, no one may enter there.'

'Porter,' said Cei quickly, 'I have a craft. Go and tell your master that I am the best polisher of swords in the world.'

The porter went into the hall. Said Wrnach: 'You have news from the gate?'

'I have, lord. There is a man at the gate who declares he can polish swords.'

'Bring him in,' was the answer. 'I have long had need of a man who could polish my sword.'

So Cei went inside all alone. He greeted Wrnach the Giant, and a chair was placed for him to sit on.

'Is it true,' asked the Giant, 'that you know how to polish swords?' His sword was brought in and laid before him. 'This sword I will give to no one, neither for price nor favour. Can you polish it?'

Cei brought out a striped whetstone from under his arm, and cleaned half of one side of the blade, and then handed it to him. 'Does the work please you?' he asked.

'Why,' said the Giant, 'I had rather than all that is in my dominions that the whole of it looked like this. It is a shame, surely, that so good a workman as you should be without his fellow.'

'Good sir,' replied Cei, 'I have a fellow outside, though his craft is different from mine.'

'Who is he?' asked the Giant. 'If he is as good as you, I should like to see him.'

'Then let the porter go forth, and I will tell his tokens. The head of his spear will spring from its shaft and draw blood from the wind, and then settle on the shaft again. Yes, Bedwyr has a wondrous craft.'

So the gate was opened and Bedwyr came inside, and there was much talk about this among the Companions who were left outside the gate. But the shepherd Custennin's son brought them all inside, and then, as though it were nothing out of the way, they crossed the three baileys until they were inside the heart of the fort itself. 'Ah,' said the Companions of Custennin's son, 'best of men is he.' And from that moment he was called Goreu [Best] son of Custennin. They dispersed silently to their lodgings so that they might later slay those who gave them quarters, without the Giant knowing anything about it.

Meantime Cei had done polishing the sword and was handing it to Wrnach the Giant, as though to know whether the work was to his liking. 'I think,' he told him, 'that it was your scabbard which damaged the sword. Hand it to me, and I will take out the wooden side-pieces and make new ones in their stead.' He stood now with the scabbard in one hand and the sword in the other, and rose above Wrnach as if he would sheath the sword in the scabbard, but instead he sheathed it in the Giant's skull and afterwards sliced off his head at a blow. After that the Companions laid waste the fort and carried off what treasure they wished. And to the very day at the end of a year they arrived back at

Arthur's court, and the sword of Wrnach the Giant with them.

(ii) The Oldest Animals

When they told Arthur how their adventure had gone, Arthur asked them which task or marvel it would be best to attempt next.

'It will be best,' they told him, 'to seek Mabon son of Modron. But we cannot hope to find him unless we find Eidoel his kinsman first, where he lies in Glini's prison.'

Arthur rose up, and the warriors of the Island of Britain with him, and soon they came to the outer wall of Glini's fortress, where Glini was keeping watch from the highest point of the rampart.

'Arthur,' he said, 'what can you want with me, that you will not leave me in peace on my grey rock? I have no treasures here, no mirth either, neither wheat nor oats in the place, without you of all men seeking to do me harm.'

'Glini,' replied Arthur, 'we are not here to do you harm, but to free the prisoner who is in your deepest dungeon. Give him up to us, and we will at once depart.'

So Eidoel was brought up out of his dark house and went with Arthur, a free man.

'What shall we do now,' asked Arthur, 'that we may find your kinsman Mabon? For that is why we freed you from Glini.'

'We must ask the birds and the beasts,' replied Eidoel, 'and maybe the fishes too.'

At this some of Arthur's men burst out laughing, and, 'Lord,' they said, 'if we are to follow courses as mean as these, it would be best for you to return to your court.'

'I did not rescue Eidoel to hear your vain laughter,' Arthur sternly rebuked them. He called on four of his men for the quest. 'Gwrhyr Interpreter of Tongues,' he said, 'it is right for you to undertake this enterprise, for you know all tongues of men and beasts and birds, and fishes too. Eidoel, it is right for you to go with him, for Mabon is your kinsman, your first cousin. And the blunt Cei and furious Bedwyr, you too shall go, for I know that whatever you two seek will be found. And first,' said Arthur, 'seek to find the Ouzel of Cilgwri.'

And so they did. 'Ouzel of Cilgwri,' Gwrhyr asked her, 'do you know anything of Mabon son of Modron, who was stolen away when he was three nights old from betwixt his mother and the wall?'

'When first I came to this place,' answered the Ouzel, 'there was a smith's anvil here, and I was the youngest of young birds. No work was done on that anvil save that I stropped my beak on it each evening, yet today there is not so much of it as a nut which I have not worn away. Yet I have never heard tell of the man you are asking after. However, what it is right and proper for me to do for Arthur's messengers, I will do. There is a creature whom God created before me, and I will go along with you as your guide to where you may find him.'

They came to the place where the Stag of Rhedynfre was. 'Stag of Rhedynfre,' Gwrhyr asked him, 'we have come to you, knowing that there is no animal older than you. Do you know anything of Mabon son of Modron, who was stolen away from his mother when he was three nights old?'

'When first I came to this place,' answered the Stag, 'there was only one tine on either side of my head, and there were no trees here except for a single oak-sapling, and that sapling grew into an oak tree with a hundred branches, and in time the oak fell, and today all that is left of it is this small red stump. From that first day to this I have been living here, yet I have never heard tell of the man you are asking after. However, I will be your guide, since you are Arthur's messengers, to the place where is to be found a creature whom God created before me.'

They came to the place where the Owl of Cwm Cawlwyd was. 'Owl of Cwm Cawlwyd,' Gwrhyr asked her, 'do you know anything of Mabon son of Modron, who was stolen away from his mother when he was three nights old?'

'If I did, I would tell you,' answered the Owl. 'When first I came to this place, this great valley you see was a wooded glen, but men came here and laid it waste. Then a second wood grew up and filled it, and in course of time yet a third; while as for me, why! the roots of my wings are become mere stumps. But from that first day to this I have heard nothing of the man you are asking after. However, I will be a guide to Arthur's messengers and bring you to the oldest creature God created in this world, and the one who has fared farthest afield.'

They came to the place where the Eagle of Gwernabwy was. 'Eagle of Gwernabwy,' Gwrhyr asked him, 'we are hopeful that you can tell us something of Mabon son of Modron, who was stolen away from his mother when he was three nights old.'

'When first I came to this place,' said the Eagle, 'I perched on a rock, and from the top of that rock I pecked at the stars each evening. It was so long ago that the rock is now not a hand-breadth in height, and yet from that first day to this I have never heard tell of him you are asking after.' As they were turning away, dismayed, the Eagle flapped his great wings wearily. 'Though once, I remember, I went hunting my food as far as the lake of Llyn Llyw, and when I reached there I sank my claws into a salmon, thinking he would be food for me for many a long day; but he was strong enough to drag me down into the depths of the lake, so that it was with difficulty I got away from him. Later he sent messengers, sewin and sea-trout, to make peace with me, and came to me in person to have fifty tridents plucked out of his back. Unless he knows something of what you ask, there is no one in the world who may. So if you wish, I will be your guide to the place where you may find him.'

They came to the place where the Salmon of Llyn Llyw was. 'Salmon of Llyn Llyw,' said the Eagle, 'here is your old friend and enemy, the Eagle of Gwernabwy, and these are Arthur's messengers. Do you know anything of Mabon son of Modron, who was stolen away when he was three nights old from betwixt his mother and the wall?'

'As much as I know I will tell you,' said the Salmon. 'With every tide I go up along the river Severn till I come to the bend of the wall of Caer Loyw [Gloucester], where I have heard such distressful outcry that I never heard its equal in all my life. And you may hear it for yourselves, if you will only place yourselves here on my two shoulders.'

Cei and Gwrhyr Interpreter of Tongues placed themselves upon the Salmon's two shoulders, and as soon as they declared themselves ready he swirled up the Severn so that all its water-meadows were flooded, and soon reached the far side of the wall from the prisoner of Caer Loyw. From the other side of the wall a great wailing and lamentation came to their ears.

Cried Gwrhyr: 'What man laments in this house of stone?'

'Alas, man,' answered the voice, 'there is cause enough for my lamentation. Mabon son of Modron is here in prison; and none was ever so cruelly imprisoned in a prison as he. Neither the imprisonment of Lludd Silver-hand, nor the imprison-ment of Greid son of Eri was as grievous as mine.' (These were the Three Illustrious Prisoners of the Island of Britain.)

'Have you hope of release for gold or silver or for worldly wealth, or by battle and fighting?'

'What is got of me,' said Mabon, 'will be got by fighting.'

When they heard this they returned to Arthur's court, to tell him where Mabon was in prison. Arthur summoned the warriors of this Island, and they proceeded to Caer Loyw and laid siege to it. But blunt Cei and the furious Bedwyr travelled on the shoulders of the Salmon, and whilst Arthur's warriors were assaulting the outer ramparts, Cei broke through the river wall and took the prisoner on his back, and they fetched him safely forth; and then Arthur returned home and Mabon with him, a free man.

(iii) The Lame Ant

Despite all these exploits, no man in the world knew where to find the nine hestors of flax seed from which should grow the white veil for Olwen's wedding day. But before the year was out Gwythyr son of Greidawl was crossing a mountain one evening when he heard a wailing and a lamentation which were grievous to hear. He sprang in that direction and there before him was an anthill red with fire. Drawing his sword, he swept it off level with the ground, and so saved its inhabitants from a death they feared beyond any other. And the one ant that was lame Gwythyr bore to safety with his own hand.

'Ah,' cried the ants, 'take God's blessing and ours, and the marvel that no man can ever perform, we will come and perform it for you.'

It was they who came afterwards with the nine hestors of flax seed which Ysbaddaden had named to Culhwch, and which they had carried off long years before; and they brought it in with none of it lacking save for a single flax seed. And the lame ant brought that in before nightfall.

(iv) The Beard of Dillus the Bearded

Not long after this, as Cei and Bedwyr were sitting one day on top of Pumlumon, in the highest wind in the world, they looked about them, and far off to the south they observed a great smoke. The peculiarity of this smoke was that it was not blown about by the wind, but stood like a pillar stright up into the air.

'By the hand of my friend,' declared Cei, 'that is the fire of no mean warrior.' They hurried towards the smoke, and while they were still a long way off they could see that it was Dillus the Bearded singeing a wild boar.

'Why,' said Cei, 'there is no leash in the world will hold the dogs Aned and Aethelm, save a leash from the beard of the warrior yonder. Moreover, it will be useless unless it is plucked from him while he is alive, and with wooden tweezers. We must wait till he eats his fill, and then, most likely, he will fall asleep.' So while they were waiting, they busied themselves making tweezers; and then, the minute Cei could hear Dillus snoring, they dug a pit under his feet, the deepest in world; and once this was finished, Cei struck him a blow heavy past all telling, so that he fell down into the pit, and they held him there till they had plucked out his beard with the tweezers. And then, once he was no good to them, they killed him.

In great joy they set off for Arthur's court, taking the leash they had woven from the beard with them. But when Cei placed it in Arthur's hand, Arthur laughed, and sang this verse:

> 'Cei wove this leash, or so says he,
> From beard of Dillus, Eurei's son;
> Were he alive thy death he'd be;
> By stealth, blunt Cei, this deed was done.'

This taunt put Cei in such a rage that it was with the greatest difficulty that the warriors of this Island made peace between him and Arthur. And though peace of a kind was made, Cei, and Bedwyr with him, would have nothing more to do with these quests, whatever Arthur's need of help, and despite the slaying of his men. Instead, they rested from their labours at Celli Wig in Cornwall.

(v) The Everlasting Battle

It was at this time, from her home in North Britain, that Creiddylad daughter of Lludd Silver-hand went away with Gwythyr son of Greidawl, the lord who saved the ants who brought the flax seed to Arthur. But before Gwythyr could marry her, along came Gwyn son of Nudd and carried her off by force. To avenge himself, Gwythyr gathered a host and came to fight against Gwyn, but it was Gwyn who won the day and took many prisoners, among them Hetwn the Leper, and Cyledyr the Wild his son; and he slew Hetwn and took out his heart, and compelled Cyledyr to eat his father's heart, by reason of which Cyledyr went mad and fled from the habitations of men.

When this news reached Arthur he was very angry. He came into the North with a host, and summoned Gwyn and Gwythyr to him, and freed their prisoners and made peace between them on these terms, that the maiden Creiddylad should remain in her father's house, untouched of either lord, and Gwyn and Gwythyr should do battle each May-calends for ever and ever, from that day till doomsday; and he that should be victor on doomsday, why, let him have the maiden.

And when Arthur rode out of the North, Gwyn and Gwythyr were in his train, and he had obtained Dumane the

105

steed of Gweddw, the leash of Cors Hundred-claws, and many another of the Giant's marvels besides.

(vi) The Tusk of Ysgithyrwyn

After this Arthur crossed the sea to Brittany, where he obtained the dogs that were named for the hunting of Twrch Trwyth. Next he went back to the North to find Cyledyr the Wild. And when he had obtained these and the rest of the men and marvels Chief Giant had demanded, he went in pursuit of Ysgithyrwyn Chief Boar, and Bwlch and Cyfwlch and Syfwlch and Cadw of Pictland went with him. When they found him in the open, Arthur himself took his place in the hunt; but it was Cadw who mounted Llamrei, Arthur's mare, and brought the boar to bay. With his big hatchet he attacked him, both bravely and often, and it ended so that Cadw split the boar's head in two and took into his keeping the tusk which was to shave the beard of Ysbaddaden Chief Giant.

(vii) The Hunting of the Otherworld Boar

Men now counted up the tasks they had fulfilled, and it seemed to them all that, hard though these were, they would prove child's play compared with the hunting of Twrch Trwyth. For this was a deed marked from the beginning for Arthur, and one likely to cost the men of the Island of Britain full dear. First Arthur sent Menw into Ireland, to spy out whether the comb and shears were still between his ears; for not even Arthur would seek to fight with him except for those treasures. Menw found the Boar in Esgeir Oerfel, and he had just laid waste a third of the country. Menw transformed himself into the likeness of a bird, and alighted down over his lair, and tried to s natch one of the marvels from off his head. But at that moment Twrch Trwyth twitched his ears, and all Menw got for his pains was one bristle, and that sharp as a sword and stiff as a spear. And when Menw wished to alight a second time, the other arose in his wrath and so shook himself that a wisp of his foam touched the bird's feathers. And from that day forward Menw was never without sickness.

Then Arthur gathered in one place all the warriors of the Island of Britain and its three adjacent islands, and the warriors of France and Brittany and Normandy came to meet with them, and many men from the Summer Country, and all with picked dogs and horses of renown. These he sent over in his ship *Prydwen* to Ireland, where there was such fear and trembling at their coming that all the saints of the country came to beg for mercy and protection. These he gave them, and in return they gave him their blessing. The men of Ireland joined with him, and they proceeded together to Esgeir Oerfel, where Twrch Trwyth lay couched, and his seven young pigs around him. Dogs were loosed on him from all sides, and the men of Ireland made an assault upon him. But though they fought with him till evening, they killed never a pigling, and Twrch Trwyth laid waste one of the five provinces of Ireland. On the morrow Arthur's warband fought with him, and they too won nothing but death and destruction. The third day Arthur himself took the field, and their battle lasted nine nights and nine days, and still no pigling fell.

'Lord,' said his weary men, 'tell us, we pray you, what is the history of this Boar?'

'He was a king,' Arthur told them, 'and for his wickedness God transformed him into a swine.'

While his men rested and saw to their wounds, Arthur sent Gwrhyr Interpreter of Tongues to have word with him. Like Menw he went in the form of a bird and alighted above Twrch Trwyth's lair.

'For His sake who transformed you into this shape,' urged Gwrhyr, 'will no one of you come to speak with Arthur?'

Twrch Trwyth only grunted, and it was his son Grugyn Silver-bristle who made answer for him. Like wings of silver were his bristles; the way he went through wood and meadow might be discerned from how his bristles glittered. 'By Him who made us in this shape,' vowed Grugyn, 'we will do nothing for Arthur. We have troubles enough of our own, we boars, without you too coming to attack us.'

'You must know,' said Gwrhyr, 'that Arthur is determined to have the comb and shears from between the ears of Twrch Trwyth.'

'Until Twrch Trwyth's life is taken,' promised Grugyn, 'those treasures will not be taken. Go back and tell Arthur that in the morning we will depart for his own beloved country and do all the mischief we can there.'

They were as good as their word, and on the morrow they swam over the sea to Wales. Arthur, his hosts, his horses, and his dogs, all hurried aboard the ship *Prydwen* and sailed in pursuit. Twrch Trwyth came to land at Porth Cleis in Dyfed and killed all the cattle there; and before Arthur could catch up with him he had killed all the men and beasts of the countryside, save for a few that fled before him.

As soon as he learned of Arthur's coming, Twrch Trwyth made off to the mountains of Preseleu, and there came Arthur too with the hosts of the world, and ranged his men for the hunt on both sides of the river Nyfer. But Twrch Trwyth slipped away from them, and reached Cwm Cerwyn, where he stood at bay and slew four champions. A second time he stood at bay there, and slew a second four champions, among whom was Arthur's young son Gwydre. And there he received his first wound from a spear, and at that drew off again.

On the morrow at point of day a fresh hunt caught up with him, and he slew Huandaw and Gogigwr and Penpingion the Roller, the three deputies of Glewlwyd Mighty-grasp the Porter, so that now he had no other deputy save Llaesgymin the Slack-hewer, a man for whom no one was ever a stroke the better. And over and above these he slew many a man of that country, including Gwlyddyn the Craftsman, Arthur's chief builder. Then Arthur caught up with him at Peluniawg, and there he slew three champions at his first onset, and two more at his second, one of whom was a king of France. He burst through their ring and escaped to Glyn Ystun, where the dogs and men lost him.

Arthur now had Gwyn son of Nudd summoned to him, and asked him what he knew of Twrch Trwyth and where he was hiding. Nothing, he said; he knew nothing. So the huntsmen moved on to attack the pigs as far as

Dyffryn Llychwr; but they were unwary in their going, and when they least expected it, Grugyn Silver-bristle and Llwydawg the Hewer burst in on them and killed them all save one, and he was deeply gored before he reached Arthur. At once Arthur turned to where Grugyn and Llwydawg were exulting, and let loose on them all the dogs that had been named for this purpose. So great was the clamour, what with barking and yelping and grunting and squealing, and the shouts of the men and the horses' neighing, that Twrch Trwyth was roused from where he rested under an oak, and he dashed up to defend them. At once he was beset by dogs and men, but by might and by main he reached Mynydd Amanw, where the first of his piglings was slain. Then a new battle was joined, life for life and death for death, and it was there that Twrch Llawin was slain. And soon a third pigling fell, Gwys by name. And when he drew off to Dyffryn Amanw, both Banw and Benwig were slain; and not one of his pigs came alive from that place, save Grugyn Silver-bristle and Llwydawg the Hewer.

From there they went on to Llwch Ewin, and when Arthur came up with them they stood at bay, and Twrch Trwyth slew Echil Big-hip and many a man and dog besides, before they withdrew to Llwch Tawy. Here Grugyn left them and made for Din Tywi, and from there into Ceredigion, with a host in pursuit of him, until he reached Garth Grugyn, where he was slain in their midst; but first he slew four champions, and dogs past all counting. Llwydawg pressed on to Ystrad Yw before he was overtaken; he slew two kings there and Arthur's own uncle, and then he himself was slain.

Only Twrch Trwyth was left now, who cut a swathe of death between Tawy and Ewyas. In his great need, Arthur summoned the warriors of Cornwall and Devon to meet him at the mouth of the Severn, and addressed them there with these words:

'Twrch Trwyth has wasted much of my land and slain many of my men. But while I am alive he shall not pass over into Cornwall. I shall run behind him no farther, but intend to join with him in battle, life for life, and death for death. As for you, do what you will.'

He made a plan whereby a body of horsemen was sent as far as Ewyas, and the best dogs of this Island along with them, and they beat the woods and the plains and meadows back to the Severn, and there waylaid Twrch Trwyth with the best of those warriors who still had life and limb about them, and by sheer force of numbers drove him into Severn. And Mabon son of Modron went with him into Severn on his dun-maned stallion, and Goreu too, Custennin's son, and the hurt Menw yelling for revenge. And Arthur fell upon him with the champions of Britain, and Osla Big-knife now drew near with Manawydan son of Llŷr, and they all closed in on him. First they dragged at his feet, and soused him in Severn till the river flooded over him. On one side Mabon spurred his horse, and on the other Cyledyr the Wild plunged headlong at him, and between them these two men snatched the shears from between his ears in a flurry of foam and a lather of white water. But before they could lay hands on the comb he found land with his feet; and from the moment he found land neither horse nor hound could keep up with him as he raced into Cornwall. Indeed it was all they could do for the rest of that day to save some of their men from drowning. Cacamwri, for instance, Arthur's body-servant, the faster they hauled him out of the river, the faster the two millstones with which he ground meal for Arthur's table, and which he always carried slung round his neck, kept hauling him back into the depths. While as for Osla Big-knife, as he went chasing after the boar his knife fell out of its sheath, so that he lost it; and then, his sheath being full of water, the faster they dragged him up and out, the faster his sheath kept dragging him down and in.

However, they were at last all dry and breathing on Severn bank, and then Arthur proceeded with the hosts of the world till he caught up with Twrch Trwyth in Cornwall. Whatever mischief was come by in seeking the shears was child's play to the mischief they met with when seeking the comb, but at last, by force and ruse and deadly stratagem, the comb was taken from between his two ears, and the hosts drove him out of Cornwall, straight forward into the sea. From that time to this no one has known what became of him, or the two dogs Aned and Aethlem, who took to the water after him. But wise men think that he couches still under a wondrous oak in the Otherworld, and Grugyn and Llwydawg alongside him, their snouts deep in acorns, and that Arthur will meet with them again when he raids the magic forts of Annwn, and not much like the meeting.

(viii) The Blood of the Black Witch

For a while Arthur lay at rest at Celli Wig in Cornwall, and bathed, and rid himself of his weariness. Then one day he rose up and said to his men: 'Is there a single one of those tasks we have not yet fulfilled? Is there a single marvel not yet obtained?'

'There is,' said the blunt Cei, 'but I will not help you find it. It is the blood of the Black Witch, daughter of the White Witch, from the head of the Valley of Grief in the uplands of Hell.'

Once more Arthur set off with a host, and Cynddylig the Guide to guide them, and they found her in her hag's cave far away in the North Country. First he sent his servant Cacamwri and Hygwydd his brother to fight against the hag. But as soon as they came inside the cave the hag grabbed at them, and caught Hygwydd by the hair of his head and flung him to the floor beneath her. At once Cacamwri grabbed her by the hair of *her* head, to drag her off his brother, but she quickly turned on him too, and dressed them down like leather hides, with many a whack and a thwack, till they crawled away squealing and squalling.

It angered Arthur to see these good servants of his almost killed, and he advanced in person to seize the cave. 'Ah, lord,' said his men, 'it will be no pleasure to us to see you scuffling with a hag. Send in the tall Amren and Eiddil.' So these two men went inside the cave. If it was bad for the others, it was a worse welcome by far that these two received, for she threshed them and thrashed them like sheaves on a barn floor, till they crept away bellowing and bawling. Indeed, no one of the whole four could have stirred from the place, had they not been loaded like mealbags on Llamrei, Arthur's mare.

Then Arthur in his wrath seized possession of the entrance to the cave, and from there he took aim at the hag with Carnwennan his knife. The blade flashed like lightning in those dark recesses, and struck her across the middle, severing her, so that the two halves stood leaning together like tubs. And Cadw of Pictland took the witch's blood and kept it with him for the shaving of Ysbaddaden.

V

Culhwch Marries Olwen

———— ❖ ————

'Are all the tasks fulfilled now?' asked Arthur.

'They are.'

'Are all the marvels obtained?'

'They are.'

'Then set forth, Culhwch,' cried the proud Arthur, 'and take your bride, as I promised you should the day I trimmed your hair in my court.'

So Culhwch set forth, and Goreu son of Custennin with him, and all those other men who wished ill to Ysbaddaden Chief Giant, and they took those marvels with them to his court.

'We are come to shave you, Chief Giant. Are you ready?'

'Where are those ruffians, my servants?' roared the Giant. 'Prop up my eyes with the forks that I may behold these treasures, the tusk, the comb, and the shears, and all things else I asked for. You cursed savage son-in-law!'

Then Cadw of Pictland dressed his beard with the blood of the Black Witch, and soon he had shaved off his beard, his skin and his flesh to the bone, and his two ears also.

'You have had your shave?' demanded Culhwch.

'Oh, oh, oh!' he bellowed. 'Yes, I have.'

'Your daughter is mine?'

'Oh, oh, oh!' he bellowed. 'Yes, she is. But you need not thank me for that. Thank Arthur your kinsman who obtained her for you. For my part, you should never have had her. And it is now high time to take away my life.'

When he had said this, Goreu son of Custennin seized him by the hair of his head and dragged him off to the mound, where he cut off his head and set it on the bailey-stake, and so avenged his twenty-three brothers. And with his father's consent, and Culhwch's, he took possession of the fort and all the Giant's dominions.

That same day Culhwch married Olwen, and she was his only wife as long as he lived.

Soon the hosts of Arthur dispersed, each man to his own country. And in this fashion Culhwch won Olwen daughter of Ysbaddaden Chief Giant, and achieved the destiny that his stepmother laid upon him.

HOW TRYSTAN WON ESYLLT

——— ❖ ———

Not long after the hunting of the Otherworld Boar, and when the kingdom had settled to rest, news reached Arthur that Trystan son of Trallwch, and Esyllt of the Whitethroat, the wife of March son of Meirchion, had gone off wandering together as outlaws in the oak-woods of Celyddon in the North, and no person with them save Golwg Hafddydd [Summer-day Face] her handmaid, and Trystan's small page, carrying pasties in a satchel and wine in a long-eared jar. For a house they had trees, and for a bed the leaves, and what with the pasties and the wine and the love they bore each other, a year was as a week to them, and the week full summer.

March came in person to Arthur to complain against Trystan. 'Lord,' he said, 'I know not what your inclination is, but you have a duty to me, for I am your sister's son and your first cousin, while he is only a cousin's son, and stands that much farther out of your regard. So avenge, lord, the insult put upon me.'

'That I may well do,' said Arthur, 'and yet he is one of the Three Unyielding Chieftains of this Island.'

'Lord,' replied March, 'it concerns your honour no less

than mine. He is your man, and it is not to be thought that he shall defy you.'

'That,' said Arthur, 'is what we shall see.'

That same day he called up his war-band and they rode north and surrounded the oak-woods of Celyddon on all sides. Trystan lay asleep, for it was the dark of the night when they came there, but Esyllt could hear the noise of arms and the murmuring of men in every bush and copse, and she so trembled in Trystan's arms that he awoke and, 'Lady,' he asked, 'why do you tremble when I am near?'

'Not in fear for myself,' she told him, 'but in fear for you. There is a mustering on all sides of the forest, and there will be men here who seek to destroy you.'

'Know, lady,' said Trystan, 'that there is a destiny upon me, that whoever draws blood from me dies, and whoever I draw blood from, he too must die. Besides, many of these men are my comrades: the blunt Cei and furious Bedwyr, Gwalchmei the courteous, and my foster-brothers at Arthur's court.'

He set her for safety in the hollow of an oak, where ivy and holly and a neighbouring yew hid her from the eyes of men, and made for where the murmuring and muster seemed loudest, with his sword like heaven's lightning in his hand, and his shield like heaven's storm-cloud on his back. And there in front of him, with an army of men, he saw March.

'Lord,' he said, 'we have a quarrel, you and I. Take your sword that we may settle it.'

But March knew of the destiny laid upon Trystan, that though he should kill him it would cause his own death, and he would not fight. Instead he called on his men to seize Trystan and bind him and bring him as a captive before

Arthur. His men, however, knew nothing of his true reason, and thought him a coward. 'Shame on our beards,' they said, 'if we fight for a man who will not fight for himself.' And Trystan passed through their midst unharmed.

A second time March went to complain to Arthur. 'Aye,' said the Emperor, 'it has gone the way I thought it would go. And now there is only one thing to do. We must send the best harpers of the Island to play to him from afar, and when his mood is softened and his heart at ease, we must send poets and praisemakers to exalt him and turn him from his anger and wrath. Then we may have speech with him.'

They did this, and when Trystan heard the sounds of harping fill the confines of the forest, so that the birds were stilled and the tree-tops silent and listening, he sent his page to fetch the minstrels to him and rewarded them with handfuls of gold and silver. Then came the poets and praisemakers, till the leaves and the branches rustled with joy of their words. These too Trystan had fetched to him and Esyllt, and to the chief song-maker he gave a circlet of gold from about his own neck, with pearls in it and precious rubies, and upon all the others he bestowed handfuls of gold and silver. And it was now, when his heart was both softened and exalted, that Gwalchmei appeared before him with a message from Arthur. So courteous were Gwalchmei's words that Trystan went with him to see his king, and Arthur bound him and March to keep peace one with the other till there should be a judgement pronounced between them.

Then Arthur spoke with each of them apart, whether he would agree to give up the lady. But neither of them would, and that was how it came about that Arthur pronounced this judgement: he awarded Esyllt to the one of them for as long as the leaves should be on the trees, and to the other for as long as the leaves should not be on the trees; and it was for March son of Meirchion to choose first.

'Lord,' he said joyously, 'that is easy for me.' And he chose to have Esyllt when the leaves should not be on the trees, for the short day of winter seems often longer than the long day of summer, and the nights are longer then, and the weeks and months pass slower.

Arthur went with his war-band to the middle of the forest and reported this to Esyllt.

'Ah, lord,' she cried, 'blessed be the judgement and he that made it!'

'Why so, lady?' asked the blunt Cei. And in answer she sang this verse:

> *'Three trees there are, both good and true:*
> *Holly and ivy and yew are they:*
> *They keep their leaves the whole year through,*
> *And Trystan shall have me for ever and aye.'*

And that is how March son of Meirchion lost Esyllt for good, and how Trystan won her for what was left of his life.

RHITTA OF THE BEARDS

❖

Long, long ago there were two kings living in Britain by the name of Nyniaw and Peibiaw, and it would be hard to say which of them was the vainer and more arrogant. One day they were walking together across a field which belonged to Nyniaw when Nyniaw said, as modestly as ever: 'I cannot think there is a bigger or a smoother field in the world than this field of mine. Did you ever see its equal, Peibiaw?'

'It is easy to see that you are no judge of fields,' replied Peibiaw. 'I have at least ten better at home. You had better come and see them some time.'

'Then my herds and my flocks,' pursued Nyniaw, pointing first here, then there, then everywhere. 'Tell the truth—did you in all your life see herds and flocks so numerous and fine?'

'Often,' said his rival. 'And they all belong to me.'

'I suspect you are a boaster,' Nyniaw reproved him, and for a while they walked on in silence. Then: 'Meet me here tonight,' he invited, as sly and satisfied as a sun-washed cat, 'and I shall show you such a field as will make your mouth run and your eyes water.'

So they met that night in the same place, with the moon at the full and a fleece of stars in the heavens.

'Look upwards,' said Nyniaw, 'to my most beautiful and extensive field.'

Peibiaw looked up, and, 'Where is it?' he asked.

'The whole wide firmament of heaven,' replied Nyniaw, 'as far as eye can reach or vision pierce, that is my wide field. Deny it,' he added; 'if you dare!'

'Why should I deny it?' asked Peibiaw, 'when I see my countless herds and flocks grazing free of cost throughout its confines?'

Nyniaw looked up, and, 'Where are they?' he asked.

'The hosts and the armies and the galaxies of stars,' replied Peibiaw, 'are my milk-white cattle and my wool-white sheep. And never,' he added, 'had herds and flocks so wondrous a shepherdess as they.'

'Who is she?' demanded Nyniaw.

'She is the moon, bland and golden, to show them where the pasture holds most nurture.'

'They shall not graze in my pasture!' threatened Nyniaw.

'Believe me, they shall,' replied Peibiaw.

'They shall not!' raved the one.

'They shall!' roared the other.

'No,' bellowed Nyniaw.

'Yes,' bawled Peibiaw.

'Over my dead body!' vowed the one, and, 'Over your dead body,' promised the other, and from shouts they came to menaces, and from menaces to brawling, and from brawling to cuffs, and from cuffs to a mustering, and from a mustering to skirmishes, and from skirmishes to war, till their kingdoms were laid waste and their armies slain, all over the grazing rights in Heaven.

News of their folly was brought to Rhitta the Giant, who at that time was king of north Wales. 'O limitless folly of men,' cried the scandalized Rhitta, 'to fight over such nonsense as that! Surely every one knows that those grazing rights are mine.' He at once assembled an army and marched against the contending remnants of the lesser armies and imposed peace upon them, and Nyniaw and Peibiaw he vanquished utterly, and to mark his disapproval of their presumption and frenzy he had their beards removed in a piece and stitched together as a cap for his head, when he went walking in the fields at night to number his sheep in the heavens.

There the matter might have ended, had not the other sovereigns who made up the twenty-eight kings of Britain taken offence at so great an insult to the two disbearded kings. 'Why,' they said, 'if once we permit this sort of thing, not a beard will be safe throughout the Island.' So they too assembled armies till their men stood thicker than wheat in a favoured croft, and the wind in their whiskers was like the sighing of summer cornfields. But it was all to no avail, for when Rhitta the Giant fell upon them he was like the first gale of autumn, stripping them of glory and strewing them over the plain. 'Why,' said Rhitta, after an upward glance, 'this looks like another extensive field of mine,' and he at once removed the beards from the twenty-five presumptuous kings, and had them stitched together as a cape for his shoulders, when he went wandering in the fields at night to count his cows in the heavens.

There it might well have rested, had not the sovereigns of the neighbouring countries heard tell of the disgrace inflicted on the disbearded kings of Britain. 'Why,' they said, 'unless we do something to stop him, this Rhitta will not leave a beard alive from one land's end to another. Besides,' the wiser among them added, 'he is quite mad, and is infringing our grazing rights in the heavens.' So they too assembled armies till their men stood thicker than trees in a forest, and the wind in their whiskers was like the sighing of autumn branches. But it was all to no avail, for when Rhitta fell upon them he was like the first gale of winter, ripping and rending them, and scattering them wide over the ground. 'Why,' said Rhitta, after an inward glance, 'we have here yet another immense, extensive field of mine,' and he at once removed the beards from the vanquished kings. 'These,' he added, pointing to the cold-chinned monarchs, 'were the animals that grazed my earth-bound pastures, and it is high time that they were driven out.' So driven out they were, with many a whack and a thwack, and Rhitta took up all the beards and had them stitched together as a mantle that extended from his head to his heels, with a good overlap in front, and a high collar to spare, to keep him warm whenever he went ambling in the fields at night to oversee his golden shepherdess.

This would certainly have marked the end of the matter, had not Rhitta heard a little later that there was a new young king in the south whose name was Arthur. By now he was so keen a beard-collector that he felt he would not know a moment's peace till he had Arthur's beard too. Also, he had been studying the design of his mantle, and it seemed to him that it needed one further patch on the hem to make it perfect. 'Moreover,' he told himself, 'it will be a kindness to the young man. If he keeps his beard, who knows but he may grow arrogant as Nyniaw or scatterbrained as Peibiaw? It is the least I can do, to preserve him from that.'

That was how it came about one day that as Arthur was washing his hands after killing a red-eyed giant in Cornwall, a messenger walked before him from Rhitta in north Wales and asked him for his beard, explaining that his master had need of it to patch his cloak, and demanding further that he should renounce all claim to the heavenly fields and the herds in the firmament.

For a while Arthur went on washing his hands. Then, 'For the second demand,' he said mildly, 'I may well promise that. As for the first, you will observe that my beard is still young. You had better tell your master to seek a beard elsewhere.'

'Perhaps he would like mine?' said Cei, jutting out a chin whose beard was like a broad black spade.

'Or mine?' echoed Bedwyr, whose beard was thick as reeds and sharp as daggers.

'Or mine?' suggested Uchdryd Cross-beard, who could throw the bristling red beard he had on him across fifty rafters which were in Arthur's hall.

'But if,' Arthur continued, 'your master is ill-pleased with my answer, I engage myself to find him just the beard to complete his mantle. Yet my advice to him is to rest content with what he has.'

This answer of his was carried to Rhitta in north Wales, who at once assembled an army and marched south clad in his mantle of beards. As he drew near to Arthur's court he saw a flashing as of heaven's lightning along the horizon before him.

'What is the light?' he asked his messenger.

'Arthur's warriors are advancing their spears for battle.'

125

Then he heard a roar as of heaven's thunder rolling through the welkin.

'What is the roaring noise?' he asked.

'Arthur's foot and his horse are greeting their lord.'

Then he and his horse were enfolded in such an odour of sweetness that wild swarms would grow tame at it and the tame swarms swoon in their hives.

'What is the sweetness?' he asked.

'Arthur's men drink mead to their lord before battle, and the virtue of that mead is that one man's stroke is as the stroke of nine, and there is no counter-stroke to oppose it.'

'We must proceed cannily, it is clear,' replied Rhitta. 'But I will have his beard just the same.'

Messengers passed between the two kings, and they met on a level plain before the armies, each with a small retinue about him.

'It is as you see,' began Arthur mildly, 'my beard is young in growth and would not cover the worn place I see on your mantle. But I think I know a beard that would serve your turn, king.'

'Whose is that?' asked Rhitta.

'Your own,' said Arthur; and the savage laughter from his chosen warriors silenced the shout of dismay from Rhitta's twelve men. 'Will you yield or fight?' asked Arthur.

His leaders of battle soared out like pillars of flame before the host, their drawn swords scorching the air, and their black chargers like thunderclouds over the plain. Where their hooves met turf the earth was a steaming cauldron; where they met flint no man's eyes might endure the fire of it.

'Lord,' said Rhitta's men, 'there is only one plan for us. You must yield.'

Then Arthur's hosts trod forward, and the sound of their tread was as the sound of the ninth wave when the sea crashed on the land and destroyed the Three Drowned Kingdoms.

'I see you tremble,' said Arthur of Rhitta's men.

'Not with fear, lord,' was their hurried answer, 'but the earth is so shaken with your hosts' tread that it is hard for a man to stand steady.'

And because Rhitta could see that his men had no use of their legs and no strength in their arms, he yielded, and Cadw of Pictland, who had shaved many a giant before, took a flaying knife with a white-horn handle and flayed off his beard in the sight of both armies.

'And now,' said Arthur, 'take an awl and sinew, king, and stitch your beard to the other beards, so that your former glory may become your shame, and your presumption your disgrace.'

This Rhitta did, and the mantle was again draped about him. And as he turned to depart, Arthur asked: 'Whose is the whole wide firmament of Heaven, king?'

'Nyniaw's, for all I care,' growled Rhitta the Giant.

'And whose are the herds of the fixed and wandering stars?'

'Peibiaw's, for all I care,' growled Rhitta the Giant.

'And who is your lord, king?'

'The Emperor Arthur,' growled Rhitta. 'And it had been better for me had you been my lord long ago.'

With that much of wisdom he returned to his own country, and his men dispersed each to his own place. He wore his mantle to the end of his days, as the badge of his servitude to Arthur, with his own beard on the lowest hem of it. This beard had been thick and yellow-white with black flecks like a lynx skin, and out of it grew a long-lasting proverb. For when a man looks out of doors on a black night of winter and sees the snow falling heavily in the darkness, if any one inside should ask him what of the weather, he will answer that it is 'as thick as Rhitta's beard'. And if any one should then ask: 'Who might Rhitta be?' this is the tale to tell him, and this is the way to tell it.

THE DREAM OF RHONABWY

❖

Once upon a time, when Madawg son of Maredudd ruled over Powys, three men set off on a mission from his court, and their journey was towards the Severn. Their mission was to their lord's brother, who had gone raiding into England, where he killed men, burned houses, and carried off prisoners. It was Madawg's command that he should do this no more, so that there might be peace between the kingdoms.

The young man who led this mission, his name was Rhonabwy. Late one evening they came to the house of Heilyn the Red, where they were to take lodgings. No one of them had ever visited there before. As they rode up to the house, what they could see was a black old hall with a straight gable end, and smoke tottering upwards from every crack and corner. But if the outside was unpromising, it was worse by far within doors. The floor where they entered was bumpy and full of holes. Where there was a bump a man could hardly stand, it was so slippery with dirt and stale water; and where there was a hole you would go in over the ankle, and mighty unpleasant it was too, for they kept the cattle indoors there along with the men. The floor had been strewed not

129

with reeds or straw, but with holly branches from which the cattle had chewed away the ends, so that the butts stood up under your foot to lame you. Nor was the main floor much better. Here they could see bare, dusty dais boards, and on one dais there crouched a dirty old crone feeding a fire, and this was her way of doing it: every time she felt the cold she would throw a lapful of husks on to the fire, which brought clouds of yellow smoke billowing upwards and outwards, so that their nostrils filled and their eyes ran, and they were expecting to choke every moment.

There was a second dais too, and on that they could see a yellow ox-skin spread. Though they did not know it, there were magic qualities in that ox-skin, and it would be the greatest good luck for whichever of them might sit or lie upon it.

They sat down as best they could near the first dais and asked the crone where they might find the people of the house. She shook her head, mumbling between her gums, and the little they caught of her words was so uncivil that they thought it best not to ask anything further. Then they heard a noise outside, and in came a man and woman, not of the handsomest either. The man was dry as last year's apple, with a twitch of mouse-nibbled beard on his up-curved chin, and his head bald as a basin. The woman had a twitch of red beard too, and was both skinny and livid, and they hadn't a tooth between them. He carried a bundle of sticks on his back, and his back was so bent that his head was little higher than his knees. She carried a bundle of sticks under her arm, and her arm was so stringy that it was like a cord binding the bundle together. They heard the men's greeting in silence, but the woman lit a fire of sticks for them and brought them for food stale bread, sour cheese, and well-watered milk.

Rhonabwy had just decided that it would be better to seek a lodging somewhere else, or even to sleep in the open, when there came a great gust of wind and rain on the roof. He judged that they were all three so weary from their day's ride that maybe they would sleep after all, and without much hope they asked to be shown their resting place.

The bald-headed, bow-backed, toothless man rose up creaking and cracking and showed them to their quarters, where there was little enough to tempt a man to lie down. The place was all dusty, flea-ridden straw-ends and branch-butts, for the oxen had chewed away everything soft from above their heads to below their feet. Over this had been spread a greyish-red, threadbare blanket infested with fleas, and over the blanket a coarse, soiled sheet in tatters, and on top of the sheet had been thrown a half-empty pillow in a grubby pillowcase. With many a groan they stretched them-selves out and tried to find sleep, and after a while, despite the fleas piercing their skins and the branch-ends their ribs, Rhonabwy's two comrades began to snore. But Rhonabwy himself could neither sleep nor rest, and lest his tossing and turning should disturb his fellows he got up and stood yawn-ing beside them. He saw the yellow ox-skin on the second dais, and thinking that it would be less of a torture to lie there than on the so-called bed, he went towards it and flung him-self down. And strange though it may seem, the minute he was on the ox-skin he fell fast asleep.

And no sooner was he granted sleep than he was granted a vision too. He saw himself and his two companions crossing the plain of Argyngroeg, and his mind and purpose, it seemed to him, were towards Rhyd-y-Groes on the river Severn.

All at once, as they journeyed on their way, he heard a great commotion behind him, and when he turned he could see a youth with yellow curly hair and a new-trimmed beard riding after them upon a yellow horse, and what was yellow of their array was yellow as the flowers of the broom, and what was green was green as the fronds of the fir-tree. So awe-inspiring appeared the rider and his steed that Rhonabwy and his companions turned to flee, but he came hard after them, and soon the most curious thing was happening, whose like no man saw before or has seen since. For such was the strength of that great charger's breathing, that when he breathed out they were blown far down the road before him; but when he breathed in they were drawn close up against his chest. This was so little comfort or convenience to the comrades that they were not at all sorry to be captured.

'Lord,' they said to the yellow-headed youth, 'in Heaven's name we ask for quarter.'

'In Arthur's name,' he replied, 'you shall have it.'

'Then since you have granted us quarter,' said Rhonabwy, 'permit us to ask your name.'

'Why should I hide it? My name is Iddawg son of Mynio, but for the most part I am spoken of by my nickname: Iddawg the Embroiler of Britain.'

'That is a nickname indeed,' said Rhonabwy. 'Will you tell us, lord, why you are so called?'

'Why should I hide it? Know then that I was one of the three envoys at the battle of Camlan, between Arthur and Medrawd his nephew. Ah, what a spirited youngster I was then! I so longed for battle and for deeds of war that I kindled all the strife I could between them. Thus, when the emperor Arthur would send me to Medrawd to remind him that Arthur was his foster-father and uncle, it was my duty to ask him for peace, lest the kings' sons of the Island of Britain and their noblemen should be killed. Arthur would charge me with the fairest words he knew, but I would repeat them in the ugliest way I could to Medrawd, so that he would reject them. That was why the name Iddawg the Embroiler of Britain was given me, and that was how the web was woven for the battle of Camlan. But three nights before the battle ended I left the field and went to the Green Stone in North Britain to do penance for seven years, and so won my pardon.'

As Iddawg finished speaking they could hear a new commotion behind them, far greater than the first, and when Rhonabwy turned he could see a youth with yellow-red hair, but unbearded and without moustache, riding after them upon a yellow horse, and what was yellow of their array was yellow as the flowers of the broom, and what was red was red as the reddest blood that ever flowed in battle. In a few strides he was up with them, and as he rode by he called out, asking Iddawg that he might have a share in those little fellows he carried with him. 'You shall have a share,' called Iddawg, 'but it is a share in protecting them.' The rider shouted his promise, and was instantly far away.

'Iddawg,' said Rhonabwy, 'who was this horseman?'

'Rhwawn Bebyr,' he was told, 'a mighty one of this Island.'

Soon they had traversed the great plain of Argyngroeg as far as Rhyd-y-Groes on the Severn. While they were still a mile from the ford Rhonabwy could see the tents and pavilions and musterings of a great host, and before they reached the bank he saw Arthur seated on a flat island below the ford, with a bishop standing one side of him and a warrior on the other, and a big auburn-haired youth before them, with a sheathed sword in his gloved hand, and a tunic and surcoat of pure black brocaded silk about him, and his face as white as ivory and his eyebrows black as jet; and where a man might see any part of his wrist between his glove and his sleeve, it was whiter than the water-lily and thicker than the small of a warrior's leg.

In their turn Iddawg and the comrades stood before Arthur too and greeted him. 'God prosper you,' said Arthur. 'Tell me, Iddawg, where did you find these little fellows?'

'I found them, lord, away up on the road.'

The Emperor smiled wryly.

'Lord,' asked Iddawg, 'at what are you laughing?'

'Believe me, Iddawg,' said Arthur, 'I am far from laughing. No, I am sad rather to find that men as paltry as these now guard this Island after the great men who guarded it of yore.'

The Emperor dismissed them, and Iddawg asked Rhonabwy whether he had noticed the ring with the precious stone in it on Arthur's hand. 'It is one of the virtues of that stone that you shall remember everything you have seen here. Otherwise, all remembrance of it would have fallen from you.'

Then they saw a troop of men advancing towards the ford. 'Iddawg,' asked Rhonabwy, 'whose troop is that yonder?'

'Those are the comrades of Rhwawn Bebyr, your protector. Mead they have and honey-ale in honour, and it is for them alone to woo the kings' daughters of the Island of Britain. That is their due and right, for in every peril they serve in Arthur's van and rear.'

On all these men and their horses he could see no other colour than the redness of the reddest blood, and if one of the riders parted from the troop he looked like a pillar of red fire mounting into the sky. And the tents in which they were quartered above the ford, those too were red.

Then they saw another troop coming towards the ford, white as the water-lily from the front saddlebows of the horses upwards, and from there down as black as jet. One rider came racing ahead, and his horse entered the ford so impetuously that Arthur and the bishop and those others who held counsel with him grew wet as if they had just been dragged out of the river. The rider was turning his horse and dragging at the rein when the youth who stood in front of Arthur struck the horse on the nostrils with his sword in its scabbard. It was a blow heavy enough to break iron, much less flesh and blood, and the horse neighed shrilly.

'Why did you strike my horse?' demanded the rider. 'Was it by way of insult or warning to me?'

'By way of warning,' answered the young man. 'And no warning is severe enough for a rider so reckless that he splashes water over Arthur and the holy bishop and the counsellors till they are as wet as if they had just been dragged out of the river.'

The rider thought for a moment and then slammed his sword back into the scabbard. 'In that case I shall take it as no insult,' he said. And straightway he turned his horse's head and rejoined his troop.

Almost at once a tall, handsome man, with bold and eloquent speech, said that it was a marvel how so great a host should be contained in so narrow a place; and that it was a still greater marvel that they should be there at all, since they had each one promised to be in the battle of Baddon by mid-day, fighting against Osla Big-knife. 'You speak true,' said the Emperor Arthur. 'Let us be on our way.' Iddawg took Rhonabwy up behind him, and the whole host set off in the direction of Cefn Digoll. When they were in the middle of the ford, Iddawg turned his horse's head around, so that Rhonabwy had sight of the whole valley. There were two troops of riders, he could see, proceeding in leisurely fashion towards the ford. One was a brilliant white troop, with a mantle of white brocaded silk about each man, and the caparison of each horse pure white, save that the fringes of both were pure black. The other was a brilliant black troop, and everything about them pure black except the fringes of the mantles and the caparisons, which were pure white.

'Iddawg,' asked Rhonabwy, 'who are the pure white troop yonder?'

'The men of Norway, with March son of Meirchion at their head. He is Arthur's first cousin.'

'And who are the pure black troop?'

'The men of Denmark, with Edern son of Nudd at their head.'

By the time Iddawg and Rhonabwy overtook Arthur's host they were below Caer Faddon. From the height they were on Rhonabwy could hear a great and terrible commotion amongst the host, and he could see how the man who one moment was on the flank of the host would the next moment be in its centre, while the man who was in the centre would be out on the flank. At the same moment he could see a rider with mail upon him and his horse come riding fiercely up, the rings of his mail as white as the whitest water-lily, and its rivets red as the reddest blood. And as he rode the whole host swirled this way and that around him.

'Iddawg,' asked Rhonabwy, 'is the host fleeing before me?'

'Rhonabwy,' Iddawg chided him, 'the Emperor Arthur never fled. If that remark of yours had reached any other ears, you were a doomed man. No, but the horseman you see there is Cei, the handsomest man in Arthur's court and his best rider. The men on the flank are closing in to see Cei riding, while the men in the centre flee outwards to the flank lest they be trampled on by Cei's horse. That is the whole explanation of the commotion among the host.'

With that they could hear Cadwr Earl of Cornwall called for, and they saw him rise up with Arthur's sword in his hand; there was the image of two serpents on the sword in gold, and when the sword leapt from its sheath it was as though flames of fire shot from the mouths of the serpents. The sight was so terrifying to mortal eye that the host settled down again and the commotion ceased, and then the Earl returned to his tent.

Next they could hear Arthur's servitor Eiryn called for, a big, rough, red-headed ugly fellow, with a bristling red moustache over half his face. The horse he rode on was as red and ugly as himself, with its mane straggling down on both sides of its neck, and a huge pack on its back. As soon as he came into Arthur's presence Eiryn dismounted and drew forth a golden chair from the pack, along with a coverlet of ribbed brocaded silk. He spread this in front of Arthur, so that all men might see the apple of red gold at each of its corners, and then he set the chair on the coverlet. It was so big that two other men besides Arthur would have room to seat themselves there. When Arthur was seated, with Owein son of Urien standing before him, 'Owein,' said Arthur, 'does it please you to play chess with me?' Owein agreed to do so, and the red-headed servitor brought gold pieces and a board of silver and set them down between the players.

They had been about this only a short time when they could see a yellow-headed, blue-eyed squire with a beard starting, coming from a white red-topped pavilion, which had the image of a black serpent at its summit, and bright red venomous eyes in the serpent's head, and its tongue flame-red. As the squire drew near he greeted Owein, and Owein marvelled that the squire had not greeted Arthur first, and did not know what reply to make to him. Arthur, who knew the reason for Owein's confusion, told him to marvel no longer. 'His message is to you. So bid him speak.'

'Lord,' said the squire to Owein, 'is it by your leave that the Emperor's bachelors and squires are molesting your ravens? If it is not, pray have him call them off.'

'Lord,' said Owein, 'you hear what the squire tells me. If it please you, call them off my little ravens.'

'Make your move,' said Arthur. And the squire went away and re-entered his pavilion.

They finished that game and had started another when they could see a ruddy, auburn-haired, keen-eyed, well-built attendant with his beard shaved coming from a shining yellow pavilion, which had the image of a bright red lion on its top. Like his fellow he greeted Owein, but Arthur was no more put out than at first.

'Lord,' he asked, 'is it against or with your will that the Emperor's squires are wounding and killing your ravens? If it is against your will, pray have him call them off.'

'Lord,' said Owein, 'call off your men.'

'Make your move,' said Arthur. And the squire returned towards his pavilion.

They finished that game and were at the first move of another when they could see a fair and graceful squire with crisp yellow hair on his head coming from a spotted yellow pavilion which stood some way off, and which had the image of a golden eagle on its top, and a precious jewel in the eagle's head. He was a noble youth, with white cheeks and hawk-like eyes, and came towards them with rage and passion, so that he might hardly speak. Even so, he greeted Owein, informing him how the most famous of his ravens had by this time been killed. 'And those that have not yet been killed are so hurt and wounded that they cannot lift their wings a fathom-breadth from the ground.'

'Lord Arthur,' said Owein, 'call off your men.'

'Move, you,' said Arthur, 'if you want to.'

'Squire,' commanded Owein, 'away with you to where the battle is hardest, and in that place raise on high the standard, and let all go thereafter as God would have it!'

At once the squire ran to the place where the battle bore hardest on the ravens and there he raised the standard. As it was raised on high, so too the ravens rose on high into the air, with passion, rage and exultation, to let the wind into their wings and throw off their weariness. Then, their strength regained and all their magic power, they swooped down furiously upon the men who had been inflicting loss and injury upon them earlier. From some they tore away their heads, and from some their eyes and ears, and from yet others they carried off their arms and legs, lifting them high into the air, and filling it with commotion, what with the fluttering and croaking of the exultant ravens and the groaning and lamentation of those men who were being slashed and gashed upon the ground. And Arthur's amazement was as great as Owein's, where they sat over the chess, listening to the commotion.

As they looked up they could both hear and see a rider coming towards them, with a gold helm on his head, with precious stones of much virtue studding it, and on its top the image of a yellow-red leopard, with two red stones for its eyes. Weary and bad-tempered, he rode to where they were seated. He greeted Arthur and told him that Owein's ravens were destroying his bachelors and squires.

The Emperor Arthur looked at Owein. 'Call off your ravens,' he ordered.

'Lord,' said Owein, 'it is your move.'

The rider retuned to the battle, nor were the ravens called off.

As they went on playing they could hear a greater tumult than ever. Men were shrieking and ravens croaking as in their strength they carried the men into the air, where they rent them and let the pieces fall lifeless to the ground. Then out of the tumult they saw a rider coming towards them, with a gold helm on his head, and magic sapphires in it, and on its top the image of a tawny lion, with a tongue like a red flame a foot-length out of its mouth, and bright red venomous eyes in its head. He greeted the Emperor.

'Lord,' he told him, 'your squires and your bachelors are now all slain, and the noblemen's sons of the Island of Britain will soon be no more. It will be hard work from this day forth to defend this Island of ours. Bid Owein call off his ravens.'

'Lord,' said Arthur to Owein, 'call off your ravens.'

'Lord Emperor,' said Owein, 'it is your move.'

They finished that game and were near the end of another, and all the time they could hear the yelling and screaming of men and the exultant croaks of the ravens, the flap of wings in air, and the crashing of armour to the ground. Then out of the tumult they saw a rider coming towards them on a huge black horse, with a gleaming helm of yellow laton on his head, with glittering crystals set about it, and on its top the image of a blood-red griffin, with precious stones for its eyes. He came riding in a rage to where Arthur and Owein sat over the chess, to tell Arthur that the ravens had destroyed his whole warband and left all Britain at the mercy of its enemies.

Arthur glared at Owein. 'Call off your ravens!' he commanded. And in his rage he crushed the golden pieces that were on the board till they were all dust under his hand. Then Owein ordered that his banner should be lowered, and with its lowering all was peace.

And even as peace was declared, there came four-and-twenty horsemen from Osla Big-knife to ask a truce of Arthur, and counsel was taken, and among Arthur's counsellors were the blunt Cei and furious Bedwyr, and Gwalchmei and Trystan and Peredur Long-spear, Gwrhyr Interpreter of Tongues, and Menw, and March too, the son of Meirchion. What was decided was to grant Osla a truce for a fortnight and a month, and then Cei arose and said: 'Let every man that wishes to follow Arthur be with him tonight in Cornwall. As for him whose wish is otherwise, let him join with Arthur by the end of the truce.'

'Iddawg,' asked Rhonabwy, 'what was the meaning of the game of chess and the battle between Arthur's bachelors and Owein's ravens?'

Before Iddawg might answer there was a great commotion of the host rising up to pursue its different ways. And with the magnitude of that commotion Rhonabwy awoke, and he was still on the yellow ox-skin, having slept three nights and three days. And because he woke just then, that is as much as men know, or ever will know, concerning the Dream of Rhonabwy.

TALES
OLD
AND NEW

■——— ❖ ———■

THE DREAM OF MACSEN WLEDIG

❖

Once upon a time, in the days gone by, there was an emperor of Rome called Macsen Wledig, who was the handsomest and most courtly of men. One day he went hunting in the valley of a river which runs down towards Rome, and took thirty-two kings, all servants of his, with him. The day was very hot, and as the sun reached its highest point in heaven the emperor grew sleepy. When they saw this, his chamberlains made a wall against the sun for him, by leaning their shields against their spears. And it was so, with his head resting on a gold-chased shield for pillow, that Macsen fell asleep.

No sooner was he asleep than he had a wondrous dream. In this dream he saw himself proceeding all alone along the river, to its source under the highest mountain he had ever known. And when he had crossed the mountain he found himself traversing a rich and level region of earth on the other side. There were wide rivers here, flowing to the sea, and at the mouth of one of these rivers he came to a great and noble city, and in the city there was a castle set all about with coloured towers. There was an immense fleet in the mouth of the river, and he could see that one of its ships was the biggest and loveliest he had ever known, built of alternate planks of gold and silver, and with a bridge of gleaming walrus-ivory connecting it with the land. He crossed the bridge and walked on to the ship, and immediately a sail was hoisted, and away she went over sea and ocean.

And still the emperor slept. In time he saw the ship bring him to a most glorious island, where he went ashore, and travelled on till he reached a land of high, rugged mountains in the west. Here, beyond a strait, lay a second, smaller island, and facing it a delightful plain, with a river flowing through it, and at the river's mouth the biggest castle that mortal ever saw. The castle-gate stood open, so he went on inside and entered the hall. Its ceiling was leafed with bright gold, and its walls were all of precious stones; the door he passed through was all golden, and so were the couches that stood on the golden floor. Only the tables were made of silver.

On a couch facing him he could now see two auburn-headed young men playing at chess, with golden pieces on a silver board. Their garments were of pure black brocaded silk, and each wore a frontlet of red gold to keep his hair in place, and had shoes of bright new leather on his feet, with gold clasps to fasten them.

Next, at the foot of the hall-pillar he saw a hoary-headed man seated in a chair of ivory inlaid with eagle-images in red gold. He wore armlets and finger-rings of gold; there was a wide golden collar about his neck, and his hair, like the young men's, was held in place by a gold frontlet. He was the most majestic-looking man Macsen had ever seen. Before his feet lay a golden chess-board, with files, and he was carving chessmen from a rod of red gold.

And then, sitting before him in a chair of gold, he saw a maiden. She was so beautiful that it was as easy to look on the sun at its brightest as it was to look on her. Her garments were of white silk, with clasps of gold at the breast; and over these she wore a surcoat and mantle of gold brocaded silk, with a girdle of gold. She too wore a frontlet of red gold about her head, only hers was studded with rubies and pearls and many sparkling stones. And the moment they saw each other, the maiden rose to meet him from the chair of gold, and he threw his arms around her neck, and they sat down together in the chair of gold; and it held them both as well as it had earlier held the maiden alone.

It seemed to the emperor that he had never known such happiness before. But it was now, when he had his arms about her and his cheek against her cheek, what with the dogs straining at their leashes, and the shoulders of the shields chiming one on the other, and the ringing of the spear-shafts, and the neighing and stamping of the horses, it was now that the emperor awoke. Instead of happiness, it at once seemed to him that he had never known such misery before, and he had hardly strength enough to stand. But when his chamberlains said to him, 'Lord, it is long past time for you to take your meat,' he let himself be helped on horseback, and rode into Rome, the saddest man that mortal ever saw.

It was this way with him for a whole week. Whenever his retinue went to feast with wine and mead out of golden vessels, he would not go with them. When they went to listen to songs and entertainment in the royal palace, he would not join them. All they could get from him was that he wanted to sleep. For every time he slept he could see in his sleep the maiden whom he so loved; but when he was awake again his life was sad and empty. And the worst thing was that he did not know where in the world to look for her.

One day one of his chamberlains spoke to him. He might be only a chamberlain of the emperor's, but in his own right he was a king, and that was why he ventured to speak.

'Lord,' he said, 'your men are all speaking ill of you.'

'Why should that be?' asked the emperor.

'Because they cannot get a word from you, neither message nor answer, nor any such greeting as men get from their lord. They think that reason enough to speak ill of you.'

'Friend,' said the emperor to that, 'summon all the wise men of Rome to me; and I shall soon tell them why I am withdrawn and sad.'

And when the wise men had been summoned and stood respectfully before him, 'Wise men of Rome,' he said, 'I have this to tell you. I have had a wondrous dream; and in that dream I saw a wondrous maiden. And unless I see her again, and soon, I care not whether I live or die.'

For a while the wise men looked at each other in silence; then the oldest of them found an answer. 'Lord,' he said, 'since you trust to our counsel, counsel you shall have. This is what we advise. Send messengers for three whole years over the three divisions of the earth, to seek the maiden of your dream. Since you cannot know which day or night may bring you good news of her, even that much hope may restore you to us once again.'

For want of better advice, the emperor had to approve of this, and the messengers were dispatched. Widely they journeyed till the end of the first year, wandering the world, and seeking tidings of the dream. But when they reached Rome again, they were no wiser than the day they set out; and the emperor now became even sadder than before, fearing as he did that he might never get tidings of the maiden he loved.

Then the same chamberlain who had spoken to him before, spoke again. 'Lord,' he said, 'I am no wise man, it is true, but why not go hunting anew in the direction you saw yourself travel before? It seems to me, some good might come of this.'

New hope filled the emperor, and the very next day he set off. Soon they reached the bank of the river where he had dreamed his dream. 'Yes,' he cried, 'it was here! And I was travelling all alone along this river to its source under the highest mountain I have ever known.'

At once thirteen men set forth as messengers of the emperor, and the wise chamberlain was at their head. They ascended the valley till they could see before them the highest mountain they had ever known. And when they had crossed the mountain they found themselves traversing the rich realm of France on the other side, with its wide rivers flowing to the sea. 'Why,' they said, 'this is the land our lord saw.'

On they went towards the sea-fords on the rivers, till at the mouth of one of them they came to a great and noble city, and in the city saw a castle set all about with coloured towers. And an immense fleet lay there in the mouth of the river, and one of its ships was the biggest and loveliest they had ever known, and planked with gold and silver. 'Why,' they said, 'this is the ship our lord saw.' And they went out to the ship across the bridge of bright ivory, and a sail was hoisted, and away she went over sea and ocean, and fetched them to the Island of Britain.

Here they traversed the land from east to west till they reached Eryri. 'Behold,' they said, 'the rugged mountains our lord saw in his dream.' Soon they saw Môn facing them, beyond the strait, and they saw Arfon too. 'Here also,' they said, 'the land our lord saw in his sleep.' And then they saw the castle at the mouth of the river, the biggest that mortal ever saw. The castle gate stood open, so they went on inside, into the hall, whose roof and floor were gold, and whose walls were bright with precious stones. 'This is the hall,' they said, 'which our lord saw in his dreams! It can be no other.'

They entered the hall, and there were the two auburn-headed young men playing at chess on a couch of gold; and they saw the hoary-headed man at the foot of the pillar, seated in his ivory chair, and carving chessmen from a rod of red gold. And then they saw the maiden.

Down on their knees went the messengers. 'Empress of Rome,' they cried, 'all hail!'

The maiden rose from her chair of gold. 'Good sirs,' she said, 'I see on you the mark of high-born men, and the badge of messengers.' For each of them wore his sleeve to the front, so that their authority would be known, and no one dare harm the emperor's men. 'Why then do you mock me?'

'We do not mock you, lady,' said the wise chamberlain. 'The emperor of Rome has seen you in a dream, and unless he may see you again, and soon, he cares not whether he lives or dies. Which will you choose, lady: to return with us, and be made empress in Rome, or for the emperor to come here and take you for his wife?'

'Good sirs,' said the maiden, 'I believe that you speak truth, but may yet be mistaken. If I am she whom the emperor loves, then it is for him to come and fetch me.'

'So be it, lady,' said the messengers, and at once took their leave. Homewards they sped by day and night, by sea and land, and as their horses failed they left them and took new ones, till they reached Rome and were shown into the emperor's presence.

'If you have found that maiden,' said the emperor, 'then name your reward. If you have not'—and he sighed—'then let me sleep.'

'We have found her, lord emperor,' said the wise chamberlain, 'and we will guide you,' he promised, 'by day and night, by sea and land, to where she waits for you. We know her name, her kindred, and her lineage, and no maiden was ever so fitted to be your empress as she.'

The emperor set out at once with his host, and with his good messengers for guides. They crossed the Alps, and France, and came to Britain over the water, and he conquered the whole Island from King Beli and his sons, and drove them into the sea. He came straight on to Arfon, and the moment the emperor saw the land he recognized it. 'This,' he cried, 'is the castle I saw in my dream!' He came straight on to the castle, and there were Cynan and Adeon, the sons of Eudaf, playing at chess, and Eudaf himself carving chessmen from a rod of red gold. And he saw the maiden of his dream sitting in her chair of gold, in garments of white silk, with a surcoat and mantle of gold brocaded silk, and a frontlet of red gold studded with jewels to bind her golden hair. 'Empress of Rome,' he cried, 'all hail!' She rose to meet him, and he threw

151

his arms around her neck, and that same day she became his wife.

Early the next day the maiden asked for her dowry, and he told her to name it. For her father she bespoke the Island of Britain from the North Sea to the Irish Sea, and its three adjacent islands, to be held under the empress of Rome. For herself she bespoke three great strongholds to be built for her in the three places she should choose in the Island of Britain. The most exalted of these she had built at Caernarvon, and they brought soil to it from Rome, so that the emperor might find health and delight there. Later she had other strongholds built at Caerleon and Carmarthen. And when they were all three completed she had high roads made from one stronghold to another across the Island of Britain. These were called the Roads of Elen of the Hosts, because the empress Elen was sprung from the Island of Britain, and the men of the Island would not have assembled in such hosts to make them for any one save for her.

The emperor stayed seven years in this Island with his empress Elen. Now it was the custom of the Romans at that time, that if any emperor of theirs should stay conquering in foreign parts for seven years, then he must remain in that conquered territory, and on no account return to Rome. The Romans now set up a new emperor over themselves. This emperor drew up a brief but threatening letter to Macsen. Indeed, all he put in it was this: IF YOU COME, AND IF EVER YOU COME TO ROME. The letter and the news of his banishment reached Macsen together, at the stronghold of Caerleon. The first thing he did was to send a letter in reply to the man who called himself emperor in Rome. And all that was in his letter too was: AND IF I GO TO ROME, AND IF I GO.

The very same day that he had this letter dispatched, Macsen summoned his host, and set off with Elen for Rome. He quickly conquered France and Burgundy, and every land that lay towards Rome, and soon he laid siege to the city itself.

But when he had been before the city for a whole year, he was still no nearer to taking it than when he started. Back in Britain folk heard of this, and it seemed proper to Cynan and Adeon to go and help their sister. So they set off with their army of Britons. It was not a big army, but the fighters in it were good enough to be worth more than twice their number of Romans. This was how it happened that news reached the emperor that a new host was to be seen dismounting and pitching tent not far from his own host, and that no one had ever seen a host handsomer or better equipped or with braver standards for its size than this.

'Who will they be?' asked the emperor, troubled.

'Who else but my brothers,' answered Elen of the Hosts, 'come from the Island of Britain to help us?'

She rode with a retinue to look at the host, and she recognized her brothers' standards. There was a great and joyful meeting between them, and then she conducted them to the emperor, who welcomed and embraced them. Soon he led them to where they might watch how the Romans were assaulting the city.

'Brother,' said Cynan to Adeon, 'when we assault the city, we shall do it more cannily than this.'

That night, when it had grown dark, they measured the height of the ramparts. Next they sent their wood-cutters and carpenters into the forest, to make a ladder for every four of their men. They had learned that every day at noon, when the two emperors went to eat, the fighting would cease entirely, and the hosts be about their meals and their business. The next morning they ate and drank early, and held their ladders in readiness, and as soon as the emperors left the field and the hosts gave over fighting, the Britons ran to the ramparts and planted their ladders against them. In a trice they were up and over, and the new emperor had not even time to snatch at his sword before they killed him, and a multitude of his men along with him. They spent three days and three nights subduing the city and its castle, and all this while they had guards at the gates so that none of the defenders should get out, nor any of Macsen's men get in.

When Macsen heard what was happening, 'I find it most strange, lady,' he said to Elen of the Hosts, 'that it was not on my behalf that your brothers conquered the city, and that they should ask no help of me.'

'Lord emperor,' she answered, 'my brothers are the wisest young men in the world. I will now go along with you, and you shall ask them to give you your city, and if they are by this time masters of it, you shall have it gladly.'

'I still find it strange,' he said, 'but we will do as you say.'

So the emperor Macsen came with Elen to ask for the city, and to ask why they had not surrendered it to him before.

'Lord emperor,' the brothers told him, 'taking this city, and then bestowing it, was a matter for the men of the Island of Britain alone. But now that it is fully subdued, do you take it, and gladly.'

With that the gates of the city of Rome were thrown open, and the emperor went in and sat on his throne, and all the Romans did him homage.

Then the emperor said to Cynan and Adeon, 'Good sirs,' said he, 'I have regained possession of all my empire. I will now give you command of my host, so that you may conquer what region of the world you will.'

So Cynan and Adeon set off, and were long years conquering lands and castles and cities, till they themselves and all the youths that were with them grew hoary-headed as Eudaf their father had been. Then Adeon became weary for his own land, and went to rule the Island of Britain; but Cynan stayed where he was, in the land which is since called Brittany.

But Macsen and Elen of the Hosts lived on in Rome till the end of their days, and of all emperors he was the handsomest and most courtly, and she of all empresses the loveliest and the most gracious. And so long as they and their children ruled, there was peace between Rome and this Island.

THE THREE PLAGUES OF BRITAIN

◆

Long long ago, in the green morning of time in this Island, there was a king named Beli the Great, who had four sons. The eldest of these was named Lludd and the youngest Llefelys, and it happened at last, when his father grew old and died, that Lludd ruled over the kingdom. No rule by a king in this Island was ever so blessed as his, for it was he who rebuilt the broken walls of London and girt it about with innumerable towers, and on these towers was such richness of colour that mortal eye had never beheld the like. And he encouraged the citizens to build great houses throughout the city, so that it might exceed in wealth and splendour all castles and cities in the realm. He himself dwelt there for the greatest part of the year, and that is why it was called Caer Lludd, which on foreign tongues became Lud's Fort or Town, and why its main gate was known to strangers as Lludd's Gate or Ludgate, and is known so still in London.

Of all his brothers, Lludd loved Llefelys best, for no man was wiser or more courteous than he. That is why, when the king of France died and left an only daughter, it was by the common consent of the kingdoms that Llefelys married her, and received the crown of France along with her, and ruled there wisely and happily so long as his life lasted.

It was in the fourteenth year of king Lludd's rule in Britain (and when his brother had ruled France for half that tally of time) that three plagues befell here whose like none in the Islands had ever seen. The first of these was a certain people called the Coranieid, who descended on these shores to cause mischief and loss. There was no discourse between men over the face of the Island, however low it might be spoken, but if the wind heard it, they heard it too. Because of this, no plan might be laid or counsel taken without their knowing about it, and to all men alive, in city and countryside, there seemed no way of getting rid of them.

The second plague was a scream which was raised every May-eve over every hearth in the Island of Britain, so wild and fearsome that it pierced the heart like a whetted spear. Because of this scream young men lost their vigour and old men their senses, and beauty and health were riven from maidens, and animals and trees turned withered, and the earth and its waters were left desolate and barren.

The third plague was this, that however great a provision was made in the king's court, even though it would be meat and drink for a twelvemonth and a day, not a bite or swallow of it would be left for their enjoyment after the first night.

Of these three plagues the first was open and its cause manifest, but no one knew the meaning of the other two; for this reason king Lludd thought it more hopeful to win deliverance from the first than from the second and third. So he had his ships made ready in secret and in silence, so that none might know their mission, not even his chief counsellors, and when the wind blew fair they left the land and cleft the seas towards France.

News of a fleet's coming was brought to Llefelys, and he at once put out from the French coast with a fleet of the same size. Then over the blue water he saw how one ship drew ahead of the others, and from mast and prow there fluttered his brother's standards of bright brocaded silk, and there was a painted shield lifted high above the ship's deck, with its point held uppermost in token of peace. He too drew ahead in one ship, and came on to meet his brother and embraced him lovingly and asked how he and the kingdom fared.

'Not so well but that we might be better,' replied Lludd. He went on to tell him of his troubles. 'And I hoped that you would know a remedy for these afflictions, brother.'

'Then we must talk out of the mouth and ear of the wind,' said Llefelys.

'How shall that be?' asked Lludd.

'I am not without a plan,' his brother assured him. And when they came to land he had a long horn made of bronze, and the one that would speak set his mouth to the pointed end, and the one that would listen to the end that was open. But when Llefelys tried to talk through the horn to his brother, there was a moaning and groaning and ruffling and scuffling inside, so that not one word came clear and undisturbed to the open end.

'How now, brother?' asked Lludd. 'Where is the virtue of the horn?'

'It is not the horn which is at fault,' replied Llefelys. 'Men, fetch me wine in pipes and cauldrons, that I may wash out the demon who thwarts us.'

They did this, and when the wine was brought they poured it in torrents through the horn, and as it burst out from the other end they had one quick glimpse of the demon holding his nose shut with one hand and dog-paddling with the other as the wine swept him headlong away.

'I think you will hear clearer this time, brother,' said Llefelys, as he once more put his mouth to the horn.

The remedy he offered his brother for the first plague, the Coranieid, was that he should take back with him certain insects from France. Some of these he should keep alive and let breed, in case he had need of them a second time, but the rest he should mash in water in order to destroy the Coranieid. That is to say, when he had returned home to his kingdom, he should summon together all the folk within its boundaries, both his own people and the Coranieid too, to one assembly, under pretence of making a settlement between them; and when he saw them all assembled he should take that magic water and sprinkle it over all of them alike. 'For the water will poison the Coranieid to the tips of their toes,' Llefelys assured him, 'but of your people it will damage toe nor tooth nor hair-tip neither.

'The second plague which oppresses your dominion,' he continued, 'is a dragon, and there is a dragon from foreign parts which attacks it and hopes to overcome it. That is why it raises such a dire and dreadful scream. What you must do is this: once you have returned home and destroyed the Coranieid, you must measure the Island in length and in breadth, and where you find the exact point of centre you must dig a deep pit, and in the pit you must set a tub full of the best mead that was ever brewed in Britain, with a silken coverlet to hide it from view. Then you must keep watch in your own person, for none but a rightful king and the lord of a true dominion will do for this, and in time you will see the dragons fighting in the shape of monster animals on earth. Soon they will rise in dragon-shape aloft in the air, and at last, when they are grown weary of so frightful a combat, they will descend in the shape of two little pigs upon the silken coverlet, and will make the coverlet sink down under their weight to the bottom of the tub. Once they are there they will drink up all the mead, then gasp out once, twice, thrice, and fall fast asleep. You must then wrap the coverlet round them, and in the strongest place you can find in all your dominions you shall bury them in a stone coffer. And I tell you this, brother, that so long as they remain in that coverlet, that coffer, and that strong place, no plague shall cross the seas again to the Island of Britain.

'As for the third plague,' he said, 'he is a mighty man of magic who carries off your provision of meat and drink to satisfy his hunger and thirst. It is by means of his magic that he causes every sentinel to fall asleep. That is why you must again keep watch in your own person. And lest that sleep of his should overcome you, you must have a tub of ice-cold water near at hand; and every time that sleep bears hard upon you, wait not a minute longer but get into the tub.'

'I will do that,' promised Lludd, as they set down the horn, 'but I must find a warm night for it, even so.' And when he had thanked his brother he took his leave of him and returned to his own country.

Immediately he had all his own folk and the Coranieid summoned to him. As Llefelys had instructed him, he mashed the insects in water and sprinkled it over all alike, and in a trice the Coranieid perished utterly, without so much as a hair being hurt among all the Britons.

A little later he had the Island measured, and its point of centre he found in Oxford. So it was there that he had the pit dug, and the mead tub placed under the silken coverlet; and it was there that he set himself to keep watch. All went as Llefelys had prophesied it would, and when the dragons had descended in the shape of little pigs and drunk up the mead and gasped out once, twice, thrice, he had them carefully wrapped up and buried in a stone coffer in the strongest place he could find, in Snowdon. And that was the end of the tempestuous scream which had made his whole kingdom desolate and barren.

When that was over, king Lludd waited in patience for a warm night of summer, and when it came he had a very big feast prepared. As soon as it was ready he had a tub of ice-cold water set near at hand, and in his own person he kept watch over it. While he was thus keeping watch, clad in arms, all at once about the third hour of the morning he heard the rarest pastime and variety of song, and felt a great drowsiness compelling him to sleep. But as his upper lashes touched the lower, he roused himself and stumbled into the tub; and from then on he went into the tub time and time again as the music and enchantment grew sweeter and stronger. The next thing he saw was a man of huge stature, clad in strong armour, coming in with a hamper and, as was his way, cramming the whole provision of meat and drink into it, and then making briskly off. And however wonderful was the pastime and song and the music and enchantment, and however wonderful the man and

162

his armour, the most wonderful thing of all to Lludd was how much the hamper would hold; for a twelvemonth's provision and a day's went into it before the big man ceased from loading. 'Stop,' shouted Lludd, as he saw him go, 'stop, will you, stop!' The big man at once lowered the hamper to the ground and stood waiting for him to catch up. For a time they fought with swords, till their swords grew blunt and useless. Then they dashed their shields one against the other till their shields burst all asunder. Then they came to grips, and fate willed that Lludd should have the victory, by casting down the oppressor between him and the ground, so that he cried out for quarter.

'Why should I give you quarter,' demanded the king, 'after the many losses and wrongs you have wrought me?'

'All those losses and wrongs,' declared the man on the ground, 'I can make good to the full extent I have inflicted them.'

'Why should I give you quarter for restitution?' demanded the king. 'You would only do the like again.'

'Not only will I never do the like again, but I will become your liegeman and serve you and yours for evermore.'

The king agreed to this and spared his life. And it was in this way that he rid Britain of its three plagues. From that time till his life's end his rule was peaceful and prosperous, in city and countryside, and the Island of Britain rejoices still in his memory.

COLLEN AND THE FAIR SMALL FOLK

— ❖ —

Once upon a time, in the days gone by, there was a saint by the name of Collen, a man of great humility though his descent was from a warrior who was not least among the mighty ones of the Island of Britain. He had a cell on the slope of a hill, and one morning he was sitting inside at his meditations when the voices of two men reached him from outside. They were speaking about Gwyn son of Nudd: the one declared that Gwyn was king of the Otherworld, with all the demons in his charge, while the other said that he was king over the fair small folk as well. Whatever might be the truth of this, whether his kingdoms were one or two, they agreed that Gwyn would be a good friend to have in this world and the next also.

Collen was so indignant when he heard this that he put his head out of the cell door. 'Hold your tongues,' he ordered them. 'Those you speak of are no better than devils.'

'You too hold your tongue,' they advised him, 'unless you want king Gwyn on your track.'

The two men went away, and Collen resumed his meditation, but only for a short while before he heard a knocking at the door of his cell and a voice asking whether Collen was at home. 'For I wish to speak with him.'

'Who is asking?' demanded Collen, who was not without some suspicion of who his caller would be.

'I am a messenger from Gwyn son of Nudd, king over Annwn and the fair small folk. It is his command that you come and speak with him on the top of the green mound at noon.'

'We shall see,' said Collen, and went back to his meditation and let not so much as a toenail stick out past the threshold all day.

On the morning of the next day the messenger came a second time, ordering Collen to go and speak with his king on the top of the mound at noon.

'We shall see,' said Collen, and let not so much as an eyelash twitch out of the window all day.

On the morning of the third day the messenger came a third time and delivered the same command. 'I speak as a friend, Collen,' he added. 'Either you go to the top of the mound this noon or Gwyn will come to fetch you. Of the two it is easier to go of your own accord and on your own two feet.'

Collen thought so too, and the hour before noon saw him climbing the grassy slopes of the green mound. He was not entirely free from fear, and thought it only prudent to prepare some holy water and carry it with him in the flask at his side. To his surprise he found at the top of the mound the fairest and largest castle he had ever seen. There was a wide parkland all round it, and throughout the parkland he could see troops of warriors in gleaming armour, and bands of minstrels with music from every kind of horn and string, and singers garlanded, and riders upon horses, and handsome youths with auburn hair and their beards just starting, and maidens tall and elegant, sprightly, light of foot and lily-handed, clad in mantles of brocaded silk, with shoes of coloured cordwain and golden bars to them; and all these people in the prime of their youth, and on every one of them the splendour that becomes a royal court.

Then he heard a voice from above him, and there on the castle's topmost tower he could see a grave and courteous man in a shining robe, who bade him enter without delay, for their king was waiting to take meat and drink with him. Squires came forward from the castle and escorted him inside, and when he had washed they brought him to where their king was seated at a golden table in a golden chair. A place was prepared for Collen opposite him, and it seemed to him that he had never beheld a man of more kingly mien and gracious manner, or of a more royal authority.

'Lord,' said Collen against his will, such was the dignity of the man who sat before him, 'the greeting that is rightfully yours be with you.'

'My greeting to you too,' said Gwyn. 'And with it the greeting of my kingdoms.'

He welcomed Collen honourably, desiring him to eat and drink. 'And if you see nothing here to please you, I have those that will fetch you every delectable thing you can wish for. Every dainty shall be yours, and all that is most delicate for the tongue and teeth; and think of what liquor or beverage you will, it shall be brought you in goblets of buffalo-horn or pure gold. Each day you remain with me there shall be new courtesy and service for you, feasting when you wish to feast, and pastime when you would have pastime. The day you depart you shall have gifts of price and horses to carry them, and at all times your treatment will be that due to a white-headed man of your wisdom. Eat then, good sir, and drink, and be merry.'

'I will not eat of the leaves of the tree,' said Collen, 'nor will I drink of the dew on the grass. And I think that you understand me.'

'Then look upon my men,' said the king, pointing to the squires in liveries of blue and red who bore dishes and napery to table. 'Did you ever see better equipment on any?'

'It is good enough, such as it is. But not for the wealth of the world,' said Collen, 'would I consent to wear those colours.'

'Tell me why,' asked the king.

'Because the red signifies burning, and the blue denotes freezing, and more I need not tell you,' answered Collen.

As he spoke he drew out his flask and threw the holy water over their heads, and in a trice all had vanished from his sight, so that there was neither castle nor troops nor men nor maidens nor music nor song nor banquet, nor the appearance of any thing whatsoever except the green mound and the noonday sun above it. Then Collen descended the grassy slopes of the mound and returned to his cell, and put his toes and his eyelashes just where he liked, and it is not recorded that they came to any harm or that Gwyn son of Nudd sent him another messenger to the last day of his age and the start of his new life in Heaven.

THE LAD WHO RETURNED
FROM FAERYE

❖

Eight hundred years ago on the banks of the river Neath in south Wales there lived a twelve-year-old lad whose name was Elidyr. It was the hope of his mother that he would grow up to be a priest, so he was set to learn his letters with a stern master. This master thought nothing of beating him till the stripes showed red and the bruises blue, so one day when he had failed to prepare his lesson he ran away up the river and hid himself in a cave where its bank was hollow. He stayed in this cave for two days. On the first day he said: 'I had rather be hungry than beaten,' and on the second day he said: 'I *think* I had rather be hungry than beaten.' On the third day, just as he was about to say: 'I had rather be beaten than hungry,' and return to face his preceptor, two little men walked into the cave with baskets of berries and jars of milk, which they presented to Elidyr, saying: 'We think it better to be neither hungry *nor* beaten.' He thought this the most sensible statement he had ever heard, and ate and drank with rapture.

'Our hearts grow tender towards you,' they told him, as they watched him wipe his mouth after finishing, 'and if you will come with us, we will lead you to a country full of games and delights.'

To Elidyr this seemed much better than facing his preceptor, and without fear or delay he followed them along a
rugged path which led farther and farther into the cave, until
at last they reached a most beautiful country, filled with trees
and flowering shrubs and adorned with rivers and rich water-
meadows. It differed from the world above only in that there
was no light of the sun and moon, so that the days were pale
and grey and the nights pitch-black. The two little men with
their empty baskets and jars led Elidyr before their king, a
stately personage as tall as no-high, who towered among his
subjects like the birch among brambles, and ruled over them
in benign majesty. He asked Elidyr many questions about his
life in the world, and promised him that he would be treated
with as much kindness as his own son. 'But though you are
free to play,' said the king, 'you will do well to learn your letters all the same. As king Solomon tells us: Though the root of
learning is bitter, its fruit is sweet. And if learning is good for
a prince, it is good for a priest too.' This also sounded like
sense to Elidyr, and he promised to learn with rapture.

For a whole year Elidyr dwelt in the Otherworld with the
fair small folk, learning his letters and playing at ball with the
king's one son. Though these men and women were small,
they were more beautiful than any he had seen before, and in
their proportions perfect. They had horses, too, and greyhounds, and other such useful beasts as we have on earth, all
of them adapted to their size. They never ate flesh or fish, but
milk only, which they made into dishes with saffron and
sweet-savoured herbs. Above all they were gentle and loving
to each other, and reverenced nothing more than truth and
loyalty. 'Good faith is our rock,' the king told Elidyr many

times. 'Let it be your rock too.' And because their way of life was so joyous and free, and so plainly superior to that of earth, Elidyr agreed, and agreed with rapture, to practise good faith to all folk at all times.

During this year the lad returned on many occasions to our life on earth, sometimes by the path he had first journeyed on, sometimes by one longer and lower, at first accompanied by the two men who had brought him berries and milk, but later quite alone, such was the small folk's trust in him. Soon he had made himself known to his mother, whose joy knew no bounds, and as his visits increased in number he told her everything he could about the manners, state, and nature of the Otherworld.

'Even their cups and platters are of gold?' she asked him, amazed.

'Even so,' he assured her. 'And the ball with which I play with the king's son is gold the whole way through.'

As she listened it came into her head and heart what a fine thing it would be for a hard-worked widow woman like herself to possess a ball of that gold, and no one on earth the poorer for its taking.

'Son,' she said, 'you love your mother?'

Of course he did, he told her.

'Then do me the kindness I shall ask you.'

Of course he would, he answered. But he was deeply grieved when it turned out to be a request for a ball of Otherworld gold. However, he had promised, and there seemed to be no shortage of gold there, nor any guard set upon it. So the very next day when he was playing with the king's son he stole the ball of gold and made for earth by the path through the cave.

He began by walking but ended by running, for he could soon hear a pattering as of mice coming behind him in the grey shade. Before he reached the light of day he knew that he was strongly pursued, and as he ran down the river bank he could see that it was his two former friends who made so quickly after him, all the time calling on him with their birdlike voices to return the golden ball. Despite their smallness they gained on him so rapidly that when he stumbled and fell at the step of his mother's house, they snatched up the ball which had rolled from his hand and held it safely between them.

'Please,' he cried, 'I did wrong for my mother's sake. That was only human.'

'We think it better,' they replied, 'to be neither faithless nor human.' And as he struggled to his feet they left him with every sign of contempt and derision.

'Take me back with you,' he cried. 'Forgive me, please forgive me!'

But they did not so much as turn their heads, and such was his shame and misery that tears blinded his vision and the little men grew blurred and disappeared through the rainbows of his lashes.

For a year after that he returned to the river every day, seeking the cave and the rough path that led out of it, but he was never able to find them. 'Misery,' he cried, 'oh misery!' and beat at the river bank till his wrists and palms were bleeding.

Yet time, which films the scar on every wound, healed this wound too, and he returned to his preceptor and his lessons, and with the passing of the years became a priest and was called brother Eliodorus. Many times and to many kinds of men, and to holy bishops too, he told of his sojourn in the

Otherworld, till he became an old, old man, with just a white fringe on top; and what impressed every listener most of all was that to the end of his days he could never reach the end of his story without shedding just such tears as those he shed the day he broke faith with his friends and lost the fair small folk for ever.

WHERE ARTHUR SLEEPS

— ❖ —

There was once a young man in west Wales who was the seventh son of a seventh son. All such, it is said, are born to great destinies, for with their forty-nine parts of man there is blended one part of Bendith y Mamau [Blessing of the Mothers, or fairies]. It happened one day that he quarrelled with his father and left home to seek his fortune in England. As he walked through Wales he met a rich farmer who engaged him to take a herd of his cattle to London. 'For to my eyes,' said the farmer, 'you look a likely lad, and a lucky lad too. With a dog at your heels and a staff in your hand you would be a prince among drovers. Now here is a dog, but where in the world is a staff?'

'Leave that to me,' said our Welshman, and stepping aside to a rocky mound he cut himself the finest hazel stick he could find. It had to be fine, for as teeth to a dog so his staff to a drover. It was tall as his shoulder and mottled like a trout, and so hard of grain that when the sticks of his fellow-drovers were ragged as straws it showed neither split nor splinter.

He passed through England without losing a beast and disposed of his herd in London. A little later he was standing on London Bridge, wondering what to do next, when a stranger stopped alongside him and asked him whence he came.

'From my own country,' he replied; for a Welshman does well to be cautious in England.

'And what is your name?' asked the stranger.

'The one my father gave me.'

'And where did you cut your stick, friend?'

'I cut it from a tree.'

'I approve your closeness,' said the stranger. 'Now what would you say if I told you that from that stick in your hand I can make you gold and silver?'

'I should say you are a wise man.'

'With Capital Letters at that,' said the stranger, and he went on to explain that this hazel stick had grown over a place where a vast treasure lay hidden. 'If only you can remember where you cut it, and lead me there, that treasure shall be yours.'

'I may well do that,' said the Welshman, 'for why am I here save to seek my fortune?'

Without more ado they set off together for Wales and at last reached Craig-y-Dinas [The Fortress Rock], where he showed the Wise Man (for such he was) the exact spot where he had cut his stick. It had sprung from the root of a large old hazel, and the knife-mark was still to be seen, as yellow as gold and broad as a broad-bean. With bill and mattock they dug this up and found underneath a big flat stone; and when they lifted the stone they saw a passage and a gleam at the far end of it.

'You first,' said the Wise Man; for an Englishman does well to be cautious in Wales; and they crept carefully down the passage towards the gleam. Hanging from the passage roof was a bronze bell the size of a bee-hive, with a clanger as long as your arm, and the Wise Man begged the Welshman on no account to touch it, for if he did disaster would surely follow. Soon they reached the main cave, where they were amazed by the extent of it, and still more by what they saw there. For it was filled with warriors in bright armour, all asleep on the floor. There was an outer ring of a thousand men, and an inner ring of a hundred, their heads to the wall and their feet to the centre, each with sword, shield, battle-axe and spear; and outermost of all lay their horses, unbitted and unblinkered, with their trappings heaped before their noses. The reason why they could see this so clearly was because of the extreme brilliance of the weapons and the glitter of the armour, the helmets glowing like suns and the hooves of the horses effulgent as autumn's moon. And in the middle of all lay a king and emperor at rest, as they knew by the splendour of his array and the jewelled crown beneath his hand and the awe and majesty of his person.

Then the Welshman noticed that the cavern also contained two tall heaps of gold and silver. Gaping with greed he started towards them, but the Wise Man motioned to him to wait a moment first.

'Help yourself,' he warned him, 'from one heap or the other, but on no account from both.'

The Welshman now loaded himself with gold till he could not carry another coin. To his surprise the Wise Man took nothing.

'I have not grown wise,' he said, 'by coveting gold and silver.'

This sounded more wind than wisdom to the Welshman, but he said nothing as they started for the mouth of the cave. Again the Wise Man cautioned him about touching the bell.

'It might well prove fatal to us if one or more of the warriors should awake and lift his head and ask, "Is it day?" Should that happen there is only one thing to do. You must instantly answer: "No, sleep on!" and we must hope that he will lower his head again to rest, by which means we may escape.'

And so it happened. For the Welshman was now so bulging with gold that he could not squeeze past the bell without his elbow touching it. At once a sonorous clangour of bronze bewrangled the passage, and a warrior lifted his head.

'Is it day?' he asked.

'No,' replied the Welshman, 'sleep on.'

At these prompt words the warrior lowered his head and slept, and not without many a backward glance the two companions reached the light of day and replaced the stone and the hazel tree. The Wise Man next took his leave of the Welshman, but gave him this counsel first. 'Use that wealth well,' he told him, 'and it will suffice you for the rest of your life. But if, as I suspect, you come to need more, you may return and help yourself from the silver heap. Try not to touch the bell, but if you do and a warrior awakes, he will ask: "Are the Cymry in danger?" You must then answer: "Not yet, sleep on!" But I should on no account advise you to return to the cave a third time.'

'Who are these warriors?' asked the Welshman. 'And who is their sleeping king?'

'The king is Arthur, and those that surround him are the men of the Island of the Mighty. They sleep with their steeds and their arms because a day will come when land and sky shall cower at the clamour of a host, and the bell will tremble and ring, and then those warriors will ride out with Arthur at their head, and drive our foes headlong into the sea, and there shall be justice and peace among men for as long as the world endures.'

'That may be so, indeed,' said the Welshman, waving farewell: 'Meantime I have my gold.'

But the time soon came when his gold was all spent. A second time he entered the cave, and a second time took too great a load, only this time of silver. A second time his elbow touched the bell. Three warriors raised their heads. 'Are the Cymry in danger?' The voice of one was light as a bird's, the voice of another was dark as a bull's, and the voice of the third so menacing that he could hardly gasp out an answer. 'Not yet,' he said, 'sleep on!' Slowly, with sighs and mutterings, they lowered their heads, and their horses snorted and clashed their hooves before silence filled the cave once more.

For a long time after this escape he told himself that he would on no account return to the cave a third time. But in a year or two his silver went the way of his gold, and almost despite himself there he was, standing by the hazel with a mattock in his hand. A third time he entered the cave, and a third time took too great a load, this time of silver and gold as well. A third time his elbow touched the bell. As it boomed, all those warriors sprang to their feet, and the proud stallions with them, and what with the booming of the bell, the jangling of armour, and the shrill neighing of the horses, never in the world's history was there more uproar in an enclosed place than that. Then Arthur's voice arose over the din, silencing them, and Cei and the one-handed Bedwyr, Owein, Trystan, and Gwalchmei, moved through the host and brought the horses to a stand.

179

'The time is not yet,' said Arthur. He pointed to the Welshman, trembling with his gold and silver in the passage. 'Would you march out for him?'

At these words, Cei caught the intruder up by the feet and would have lashed him against the wall, but Arthur forbade it and said to put him outside, and so Cei did, flinging him like a wet rabbit-skin from the passage and closing the stone behind him. So there he was, without a penny to scratch with, blue as a plum with fright and bruises, flat on his back in the eye of the sun.

It was a long time before he could be brought to tell his story, and still longer before he grew well. One day, however, he returned, and some friends with him, to Craig-y-Dinas.

'Where is the hazel tree?' they asked, for it was not to be seen. 'And where is the stone?' they asked, for they could not find it. When he persisted in his story they jeered at him, and because he might not be silenced they beat him, and so it came about that for shame and wrath he left the countryside for ever. And from that day to this no one, though he were seven times over the seventh son of a seventh son, has beheld Arthur sleeping with his host, nor till the day of Britain's greatest danger shall any so behold him. So with the hope that that day is a long way off, we reach the end of our story.

THE AGED INFANT

❖

At a farm-house in the parish of Llanfabon, near the eastern bound of Glamorgan, there lived some hundreds of years ago a young widow woman and her infant son. He was three winters old, Griff by name, and well-grown for his age, and no mother and child in the kingdom were more fond of each other than they. Now it happened that Llanfabon was a parish packed to the seams with fairies or Bendith y Mamau, as they were called; and these fairies were famous beyond most for two things: their immoderate ugliness and their love of mischief. Of all their tricks there were two which pleased them most: they would lead men forward with their songs and music till they were neck-deep in bog or swimming in a pond, and they would steal children from the cradle neater than you or I would lift a nut from its shell. No wonder, then, that the young widow kept a close watch on her son, and that she loved him the more dearly for the perils that beset him.

But what must be will be, come wind or high water. One day she was warming Griff's broth in the kitchen when there arose a moaning and groaning from the cow-house, as though a beast were in pain or at point to die. Quickly she pushed the broth from the fire and ran that way, but except that the cows were restive and their head-ropes trembling, she could find nothing amiss. But what was her grief and horror when she returned to the kitchen to see no trace of her son. She ran to the loft: not a soul was there. She ran back to the kitchen; not a soul could she see. Indoors and out there was nothing but nothing.

All that afternoon she searched the farm and its grounds. 'Griff!' she cried here, and 'Griff!' she cried there, but for all her searching and crying she found neither boot of him nor button. It was towards sunset, as she sat tired at home with her apron over her head, that she heard a noise at the door. She looked up with a cry and saw a little fellow there, watching her.

'Mother!' he said. One word and no more.

She watched him in her turn, from the topmost hair of his head to the soles of his red shoes. Slowly she shook her head. 'You are not my Griff.'

'I am,' said he, 'to be sure.'

He looked as like her Griff as one lamb to another (though no lambs look alike to the ewes that feed them). So, lest she should make some mortal mistake, she brought him inside and fed him with Griff's broth, and acted from then on as though he was none other than her son. Yet all the time there was unease in her mind. For one thing, he got no bigger, whereas Griff grew out of his clothes every season; and for another, he showed daily more ugly, whereas Griff was as handsome as paint. At last she resolved to visit the Wise Man of Castell-y-Nos and take his advice in the matter.

'You have come to the right man,' he told her, when he had listened to her story and asked her twenty-one questions, 'and if you follow my instructions your troubles will soon be over. At the stroke of tomorrow's noon take a hen's egg and cut it through in the middle. The one half you must throw away, but hold the other in your left hand, and with your right you must stir it and mix it, backwards and forwards, for some time. Let the little fellow see what you are up to, but on no account call his attention to it. It is my hope that he will then ask you what you are doing. If he does, reply that you are mixing a pasty for the reapers, and should he make an answer to that, then that answer is what I want to hear.'

The woman returned home, and at noon on the morrow she followed the Wise Man's instructions in every detail. She could see the little fellow keeping his eye on her as she threw away half the egg and went on mixing the rest in its shell. His face looked rather darker as, 'Mother,' he asked, 'what are you mixing in the egg-shell?'

'I am mixing a pasty for the reapers, boy.'

'Oh,' he said, 'is that it?' and spoke a verse:

> '*I saw the acorn before it was made an oak,*
> *The egg I saw before it was made a hen;*
> *But never saw I woman mix and cook*
> *Such egg-shell pasty for her reaping-men.*'

As he said this, he looked so cross and ugly that she could hardly bear to see him.

That same afternoon she went again to Castell-y-Nos and informed the Wise Man of all that had happened. 'No question of it,' he told her, 'your little fellow is one of the Bendith whom they have put out with you to rear. Why, if he saw the acorn before it was made an oak, he must be three hundred

years old at least. Now the next full moon will be in four
nights' time; and this is what I want you to do. By twelve that
night you must go to the place where four roads meet beyond
the ford, and once there you must so hide yourself that you
will see everything and nothing see you. It may well happen
that on one of those four roads, or up and down the river, you
will see something that will tempt you to rush out or cry
aloud, but I give you timely warning: make the slightest move,
so that you are discovered, and you shall never see your own
true son again.'

The woman returned home, greatly troubled in mind, neither knowing what the full moon would bring forth, nor
assured that she could trust to the Wise Man's counsels, for
she was not given to midnight perambulations at the best of
times, and this clearly was one of the worst. However, her
longing to see her true son Griff and her disgust at the little
fellow who had taken his place hardened her resolution. At
the appointed time, on the fourth night, she went to where
the Wise Man had directed, dressed in a black cloak and with
a shawl to cover her head and face. There was a large and
leafy bush on the rising ground near the ford, and she crept
quietly up behind this and waited for midnight. For a time
there was silence, and then a fox barked over the hill. Then a
longer silence till the owl tu-whooed near the river. Then into
the silence that followed there entered the faint sound of
music, of fiddle and harp and small voices, coming from afar
and drawing near to the ford. Resolutely she fought sleep
from her eyes, though the music impelled her to slumber, till
at last she could see them coming along the road from the
north, tiny men in red cotton hats and women in skirts of

blue and green, some dancing light as linnets, and others with parasols or stringed instruments. Soon they were passing her in hundreds, and in the middle of the procession, walking between four of the Bendith who appeared to keep guard on him, whom should she see but Griff, her own lost child, taller by a year's growth—but thin, she thought, and worn.

At that sight she so far forgot herself as half to rise, so that she might rush forward and free him, but luckily the same owl tu-whooed near the river, the Wise Man's warning echoed in her mind, and she shrank down once more behind the bush. A few minutes and the procession had all passed. For a while still she saw moonlight stroke the red cotton caps and skirts of blue and green, and heard the music and voices raised in fairy song; then sight and sound of them died in the south, and she rose to her feet and walked quickly back to her cottage.

In the morning it was all that she could do not to show her loathing of the little fellow at home as he came for his breakfast and to have his head combed. Every time he called her 'Mother' she felt quite sick at him. But there was too much at stake for mere temper to rule her, and to the little fellow's eyes and ears she looked and sounded as deceived and devoted as ever. Before the morning was out she was on her way to the Wise Man's, and so certain was he of his wisdom that she found him sitting on the wall waiting for her.

'Yes,' he told her, when he had heard her story and asked his twenty-one questions, 'you came to the right man when you came to me. I have read the signs right so far, and now I will read them right once more. This is what I want you to do. You must search the whole parish for a black hen, black all over. I expect you have many a time roasted a hen with its feathers off; but this time I want you to roast it with them on. So place it before your fire on a flat dish the minute it is killed, and then close every hole and cranny in your cottage save where the smoke goes out through the roof. Let the little fellow see what you are doing, but on no account call his attention to it. Nor should you appear to take much interest in what he may do. But once the hen is done to a turn, so that every feather falls off on the dish, then is the time to keep an eye on him!'

This sounded more than a little strange to the mother, but he had been proved right twice already, and she thought it likely he would be proved right this time again. The very next day she went looking for a black hen, and was not much surprised to find nothing of the sort among her own gay scratchers. During the next two days she walked north and south through the parish, and during the next two days east and west, but without finding a black hen black all over.

There was now only one farm left. And as she walked towards it she could see the housewife running in and out of the farm with an empty sieve, and every time she ran in she threw her apron over the sieve as though to keep something inside it, and the moment she was inside she would turn it upside down with an emptying motion on to the floor.

'Woman alive,' she asked, 'what are you doing?'

'I'm trying to fetch a little sunshine into the house,' she called back, 'only I'm not doing very well at it. Outside I have a whole sieveful, but by the time I get back in I lose it every morsel. I'd give a black hen, black all over, to the woman who could fetch the sun inside for me.'

It seemed to the mother that this must be the Wise Man's

joke on her, but she unhesitatingly walked inside and took down the shutters, so that the sunshine poured all over the floor, and then in no time at all she was walking homewards with feet light as eggshells and a black hen under her arm.

At her own farm she at once made up the fire and killed the hen, fully aware that the little fellow was watching her with eyes as sour as crab-apples. Then she placed the hen on its flat dish before the fire. Strange though it may sound, she was so wrapt up in what was happening to the hen that she had no eyes for the little fellow, and as the feathers began to fall out one by one she forgot his very existence. As the last feather left the hen there was a burst of music from outside the house, much like that she had heard when she was in hiding near the cross-roads. She looked wildly about her, but of the little fellow she could now see neither boot nor button. At the same moment she heard the voice of her own lost child calling, 'Mam, mam!' from somewhere outside. Running to the door, she flung it open, and there he was, standing in the yard, tall and thin and worn, just as she had seen him among the fairy host.

He seemed puzzled by the passion of her greeting, and it was not until she asked him where he had been so long that she knew why.

'Not long, is it, Mother?' he asked. 'I stayed only a minute to listen to the music.'

And for all his year's sojourn with the fair small folk, that was as much as he could tell her. And because that is as much as anyone can tell, we have now reached the end of our story.

THE WOMAN OF LLYN-Y-FAN
I
The Meeting

———— ❖ ————

Once upon a time, in the days gone by, a man and his wife lived at the farm Blaensawdde in the shire of Carmarthen in south Wales. It was not by farming, however, that the husband maintained himself, but by combat and wars; and as often happens to those who follow the wars, he was killed, and three of his four sons with him. A fourth son of his was too young to carry arms, and when news of her affliction reached his mother, 'War shall not take away my fourth,' she vowed, and she kept the boy close to her skirts and set him to learn only those arts which a farmer should know.

He was busied with this till there was none throughout the countryside more skilled than he in crops and weather and the care and pasturing of beasts. By this time too he was a man in feature, form, and favour, and as handsome a youth as mortal ever saw.

'Mother,' he said one day, 'is it not time for me to take a wife?'

'What wife shall that be?' she asked him.

'That,' he confessed, 'is what I do not know.'

No long time after this it happened that he drove his cows up on to the mountain, and because the sky was blue and the sun at its zenith, he sat down for a while by the lake there, and what with the warmth of the air, the sweet smell of the beasts, and the water lapping the lakeside, he fell from thinking to musing, then from musing to drowsing, and from drowsing declined into a dream-filled slumber. He had been sleeping for as long as it takes the sun to move one handbreadth through Heaven when he thought he heard a voice calling on him to awake, with this form of words:

> *'In drowsing and dreams*
> *Naught's what it seems;*
> *All's an illusion*
> *That grows from delusion.*
> *If your true love you'd see,*
> *Then see her in me;*
> *So quick, lad, awake,*
> *And look on the lake.'*

In a trice he sat up, shaking his head and rubbing his eyes, and there, seated before him on the surface of the lake, he saw a maiden so beautiful that no lady of the olden time, though they were queens of the world and lovely as seashells, might equal, much less excel, her.

She was combing her hair with a comb of bright gold, and so golden was the maiden's hair that he could not tell what was hair, what was comb, what was sunlight. Her neck was whiter than the foam of the wave, and her palms and her wrists like the snow that falls on Christmas morning. Her eyes' blue was the blue of bugloss, and the mouth on her red as the reddest foxglove. And because the air was still and the water smooth, he could see her as in a mirror, in two images above and below; and nothing under Heaven's vault was more lovely than the water-image save the image glowing in air.

'Maiden,' he cried, and, 'Lady!' but could say no more for fear he should frighten her away. But because she stayed smiling before him, he went to the water's edge and held out his hands, offering her the crusted bread and goat's-milk cheese which his mother had prepared for him to eat on the mountain. At this she came gliding nearer, but only to shake her head and grimace at what he offered, and the voice he had heard in his dream came from between her lips, saying:

> *'Too hard is your bread:*
> *Not with that I'll be fed.'*

Hardly had the last word left her lips when she plunged quickly under the surface of the water, leaving him sorrowful and alone. He waited till the lowing of the cattle announced that it was time to make for home, but she did not appear again, and when he descended the mountain he walked slow as beetle and looked bemused as the moon-eyed cows.

'Why, son,' asked his mother, the moment her eyes beheld him, 'what has befallen you?'

He told her his story in full, even showing her what hard-baked bread he had left.

'True, son, I baked the bread harder than I use, and it was not to be expected that a queen among maidens should break her white tooth on it. But never fear,' she promised him, 'all that is wrong can be mended before the boots go under the bed.'

Without more delay she mixed dough and firmed it slightly in the oven. In the morning he went to the mountain with his cattle, and, by the time the sky was at its bluest and the sun burning overhead, was seated by the lakeside, waiting for the maiden to appear. But though minute followed minute and hour upon hour, there was no more sign of the maiden than if she were the creature of a dream. At last, however, he noticed how his cattle would keep making their way to the mountainous far side of the lake, though the grazing had always been poorer there. He hurried after them, and as he was scrambling along the slope, whom should he see but the maiden, seated on the water combing her golden hair.

'Maiden,' he cried, and, 'Lady!' and this time he had courage to continue when he recalled with what smiles she had looked at him the day before. 'Is there anything on earth can bring you from the lake to live with me?' At the same time he held out his hands, offering her the unbaked bread and ewe's-milk cheese his mother had prepared for him to eat on the mountain. But this time too she grimaced, saying:

> *'Too soft is your bread:*
> *Not by that I'll be led.'*

And no sooner had the last word left her lips than she plunged so slowly under the surface of the water that the ripples hardly noticed she was gone.

'Well, son,' asked his mother as he returned home towards nightfall, 'what has befallen you this time?'

He told her his adventure in full, even showing her what unbaked bread he had left.

'True, son, I made the bread softer than I use, and it was not to be expected that a queen among maidens should soil her red tongue on it. But never fear,' she promised him, 'all that is wrong can be mended before the boots go under the bed.'

Without more delay she mixed dough and baked it in a crimson-ash oven till bread came forth of such perfection that neither mother nor son had ever beheld the like. In the morning he once more drove the cattle to the mountain and seated himself by the lakeside, but for long there was no more sign of the maiden than if she were a creature of gossamer and mist. As evening fell he began to collect the cattle, and with heavy feet prepared to leave the mountain. Luckily he took one last look over his shoulder, and there to his delight saw the maiden seated on the lake as calmly as ever, combing her golden hair. He ran joyously towards her, and, 'Maiden,' he cried, 'Lady! Unless you love me, it is no better for me to live than to die.'

'A pity,' she said, 'to cause the death of a handsome young lad like you. But it would be wrong of me to keep you when you are in such a hurry to depart.'

'Lady,' he pleaded, 'a minute to you was an hour to me. Is there anything on earth can bring you to marry me?'

As he said this he held out to her the true-baked bread and cow's-milk cheese his mother had prepared for him to eat on the mountain. This time, to his delight, she nodded and said:

> *'True-baked is your bread:*
> *And with that I'll be wed.'*

'But remember,' she added, as he jumped for joy on the bank, 'that if during our wedded life you strike me three causeless blows, you shall lose me straightway and for ever.'

Hardly had she finished speaking when, with a sign to him to stay where he was, she plunged beneath the surface of the water. Hardly had he kissed the nearest cow for happiness when she returned, bringing with her a hoary-headed man of great dignity and stature, in a mantle of white brocaded silk with jewelled brooches on each shoulder, and a second maiden so like herself that it might have been her image in the water come to life and walking at her side. No two roses and no two pearls were ever so alike as they, and he stared from one to the other in consternation, wondering which was the maiden he loved best, and which her sister of a birth.

'Am I told truth, lad,' asked the hoary-headed man, 'that you want to marry one of my daughters?'

'Unless she loves me,' he replied, 'it is no better for me to live than to die.'

'A pity,' said the hoary-headed man, 'to cause the death of a healthy young lad like you. Just tell me which of my daughters it is that you love, and my consent will not be hard to win. Speak now: she on the right or she on the left?'

'I think,' he began, and then fell dumb as a doorknob.

'Speak louder, lad,' advised the hoary-headed man. 'I cannot hear you.'

'I think,' he began, and fell dumb as a doorknob again.

'Either you grow dumb, lad, or I grow deaf. Louder!' said the hoary-headed man.

It was at this desperate moment that one of the sisters thrust her foot a little forward, so that it slid into sight from under her mantle. It was a movement slighter than when a sleeping bird stirs a feather or a cat a hair, but not so slight that he did not notice it, and notice too that her sandal was tied with a wide, not a narrow tie, and its lace folded even as he had seen it earlier when only she was on the surface of the lake.

'This,' he said briskly, 'is the lady I love best.'

'Your choice is a good one,' agreed the hoary-headed man, 'so let us now discuss the dowry. What I am willing to give is this: as many sheep, cattle, goats and horses as she can count without drawing her breath anew. But I give warning, that if during your wedded life you strike her three causeless blows, you shall lose her straightway and for ever.' And because he was as wise as he was hoary-headed, he added: 'And lose the dowry too.'

At his signal, the maiden whitened her knuckles and tightened her eyes, and drew in the mightiest breath that any one ever heard, and this was the way she counted: 'One-two-three-four-five, One-two-three-four-five'—and continued counting in fives faster than a fly's wing-beat till she was bent in her doubles and the breath all out of her. When she had counted the sheep she counted the cattle, and after the goats the horses, and long before she finished, her father's face grew grave. But because his word was his word, and a very good word, he did not hesitate before bending down to the surface of the lake and chanting this verse aloud:

> 'Spotted cow that's light and freckled,
> Dotted cow with white bespeckled,
> Mottled cow so brightly deckled,
> Wend earthwards now.'

In this same fashion he called on the sheep and the goats and the horses, and what a wondrous sight that was, to see them come splashing out of the lake and stand booing and baaing, yeaing and neighing, in a tumultuous, spray-shaking throng.

Then the fond farewells were taken and the tears of

parting shed, and before an eye might be dry again the hoary-headed man and his remaining daughter sank from sight beneath the surface of the water. The ripples had not forgotten them when the lady of the lake came to join her sweetheart on the shore, and he saw that the earth was as easy to her as the water had been. As the shadows lengthened on the lake they left the mountain, and all that wealth of dowry with them, and the lad's own cattle too. And before moontime and owl-light took over the land, they reached his mother's farm at Blaensawdde, where in no time at all they were married, and in hope to live happily ever after.

II
The Parting

———— ❖ ————

Now season followed season and year upon year till their marriage was blest with three fine sons. By this time they lived at Esgair Llaethdy, six miles from the lake, and their joy and prosperity looked like lasting for ever—except for the threat of the three causeless blows.

It happened one year about egg-hatching time that there was a christening among the neighbours which they had promised to attend. But husband and wife were not of one mind about this, for she thought the house too distant and the road uphill, and though in the end she agreed to go with him, she was slow and reluctant in all her preparations.

'Wife, wife,' she heard him calling, 'are you not ready yet?'

'I shall still be ready sooner than I wish,' she retorted.

The next minute he came bustling out-of-doors. 'Where are the horses?' he reproached her. 'Unless you meant it, why promise to bring them to the door?'

'I shall bring them in good time,' she told him, 'if first you go back indoors and fetch me the gloves I left there.'

Because time was short he ran back in and came quickly out with the gloves. To his vexation she was standing exactly where he had left her. 'Get along, wife, get along!' he urged; and when she still made no move, he tapped her lightly on the arm to hurry her up.

'You forget your manners, husband,' she reproved him, 'and you forget what is not less important. What of your promise and the three causeless blows? The first is now struck. Pay more heed to the second!'

From that warning he saw how he must be very careful indeed, if so unmeant and so unhurtful a tap as that should count as a causeless blow. But it happened one year about nest-building time that there was a wedding among the neighbours which they had promised to attend. It was the happiest assembly, the bride like a linnet and her groom handsome as gorse, but when the merriment and good wishes were at their highest he was astonished to see his wife burst into a fit of weeping.

'Wife, wife,' he urged, tapping her arm, 'is this a time for weeping?'

'I weep,' she told him, 'because their troubles are now beginning. And so are ours too, for this is the second causeless blow.' And as she left the house in tears, she called back to him: 'Pay more heed to the third!'

From that day forth they vowed to be even more careful than before, for only one blow now remained to them, and that might be so easily given, in jest or forgetfulness. But it happened one year about nest-flushing time that there was a funeral among the neighbours which they had promised to attend. All was black and tearful there, but when the grief was at its deepest he was astonished to hear his wife burst into a fit of laughter. He raised his head, frowning, but all she did was laugh louder and yet louder, as though it was past her power to stop.

'Wife, wife,' he urged, tapping her arm, 'is this the place for laughter?'

'I laugh,' she told him, 'because the dead man's troubles are over. And so is our marriage too, for this is the third causeless blow.' And as she left the house, she called back to him: 'Farewell, husband, for ever!'

Quickly she made for the farm at Esgair Llaethdy, where she called all her animals together, those that had come out of the lake so long ago and all their progeny. First she called the cows:

> *'Spotted cow that's light and freckled,*
> *Dotted cow with white bespeckled,*
> *Mottled cow so brightly deckled,*
> *Plod homewards now.'*

When the cattle heard her calling they came in from the fields and out from the byres, and four oxen at plough plodded to her with their plough behind them; and a little black calf just slaughtered came down off the hooks and ran to her, crying.

Then she called the sheep:

> *'Kerry sheep long held in fold,*
> *Merry sheep dong-belled with gold,*
> *Fairy sheep song-spelled of old,*
> *Drift homewards now.'*

When the sheep heard her voice they ran to her from the folds and the walled pastures, the ewes with their lambs, the rams with their curly horns, and the brave bellwether at their head, bawling.

Then she called the goats:

> *'Goat on high that's dry of coat,*
> *Goat with eye so sly to note,*
> *Goat whose cry is wry in throat,*
> *Skip homewards now.'*

The goats came skipping from the copses and leaping from the rocks, their beards a-wag and their ears held high. And when they pressed bleating about her she called to the horses:

> *'Horses tall and gay and bobtailed,*
> *Horses small and bay and lobtailed,*
> *Horses all, though grey and hobnailed,*
> *Clop homewards now.'*

At once they surged whinnying round her, their noses hollowing her hands, their hooves going clop, and their tails a-swish and a-sway. And when all these creatures were assembled in hosts they set off behind her for the lake of Llyn-y-Fan. They went, we are told, not in silence, but with the voices of joy proper to their kind. At their head walked the black bull of Esgair Llaethdy with weaving horns and nostrils red and steamy; and behind them three white stallions with whistling manes whose sandals clashed and thudded. And leading the bull was the woman of Llyn-y-Fan, with the little black calf beside her, quiet now and sucking at her thumb.

As moontime and owl-light took over the land they reached the lake, and a wondrous sight it must have been to see them splashing into the water, their backs flaked with quicksilver, and the lake healing over them, and the ripples forgetting the place, till of all that host of creatures not a trace remained save the furrow scraped by the plough the four oxen drew, and the hoofmarks in the dust of the road.

III

The Sequel

———— ❖ ————

I n this fashion the woman of Llyn-y-Fan came from and returned to the Otherworld, and this would be the end of her story were it not for the three sons she left behind her, who were now full-grown young men. For while her husband knew by the destiny upon him that he had lost her for ever, the sons did not lose hope of seeing her again. One day that hope was rewarded: the eldest son was passing the gate known ever afterwards as the Physician's Gate when his mother appeared before him and instructed him that he had a great work to do in the world.

'What work is that, mother?'

'To heal the sick and tend the helpless,' she told him.

'Gladly, mother,' he answered, 'and so would my brothers do, had we the knowledge how.'

At this she handed him a satchel filled with recipes and prescriptions. 'Here is knowledge for thirty, much less three.' That was how these three brothers became the most skilled healers of the sick in Wales, and are known to this day as the Meddygon Myddfai, the Physicians of Myddfai. In that family there have been healers for eight hundred years, all with good fingers and good hearts. And that is the end of her story.

EIGHT LEAVES OF STORY

I

The Three Staunch Swineherds of Britain

———— ❖ ————

These are the Three Staunch Swineherds of the Island of Britain:

Pryderi son of Pwyll, who minded the swine of Pendaran Dyfed his foster-father. These swine were the seven pigs brought by Pwyll from the Otherworld, and the place where he minded them was Glyn Cuch in Dyfed. And when Gwydion son of Dôn carried off the pigs by guile and magic, Pryderi pursued him into the fastnesses of north Wales, and there lost his life.

Trystan son of Trallwch, who minded the swine of March son of Meirchion, while the swineherd carried his message to the lady Esyllt, March's wife. Arthur and March, Cei and Bedwyr and the courteous Gwalchmei, came against him with armies, but for all their pains won never a porker, by force, by fraud, or by theft.

Coll son of Collfrewi, who minded the sow Henwen [Old-white] in Cornwall. At the headland of Awstin she took to the sea like a fish, with Coll gripping on to her bristles whichever way she went by sea or by land. At Maes Gwenith [Wheat-field] in Gwent she dropped a wheat-grain and a bee, and ever since that is the best place in Wales for wheat. From Gwent she proceeded to Dyfed and dropped a barley-grain and a bee, and ever since that is the best place for barley. From Dyfed she sped north to Eryri [Snowdon] and dropped a wolf-cub, an eaglet, and a kitten. Coll flung the kitten into Menai Strait, but it swam to land as sleek as a seal and became Palug's Cat, and so won fame as one of the three plagues of Môn and a sworn foe to Arthur, and for long was a mangler of his men till Cei polished his shield and marched against her.

II

The Sigh of Gwyddno Long-shank

———— ❖ ————

In those far-off days before the sea overflowed the kingdoms, Gwyddno Long-shank was king over Cantre'r Gwaelod, the Low Country in the west. Of all the kingdoms of Britain this was by so much the best that any acre of it was worth the best four acres that might be coveted elsewhere. In all its length and breadth there was only one fault to be found with it: it lay lower than the level of the sea. That was why a great wall had been built to protect it, with watergates and sluices, so that at low tide the rivers might run out, but at high tide no sea might get in. To patrol this wall and open and shut the sluices was, after the kingship, the most important office of the country, and at the time we tell of it had been entrusted to prince Seithenin of Dyfed. He was a man gallant, handsome and gay, but he was also one of the Three Arrant Drunkards of the Island of Britain.

One night in the month of high tides there was a feast in the royal court, at which meat and drink without limit were served from Gwyddno's hamper of plenty. As the evening wore on a fierce gale leapt out of the south-west, so that the waters were rolled into the narrow passage between Wales and Ireland. Never was there more need of a watchman, and never was Seithenin more drunk. Because of his negligence the sluices were not closed and the water-gates stood open, so what began as a trickle ended as a flood, and by daybreak the whole country and its sixteen cities were under the wave. From that day till this the sea has held rule over Cardigan Bay, but where at low tide one sees tree-stumps or a stone wall, or hears the ringing of water-swung bells, those are what is left of Gwyddno's rich kingdom.

Gwyddno himself escaped with his court to high ground, and a few of his subjects with him, and they made for those mountains of the north which were empty and desolate. There they maintained themselves by toil and hunting, and no men had ever a life more hard than they. Of them all it was natural that Gwyddno should feel their loss most keenly. From a proud king he became a poor squire, and maintained himself by a salmon-weir on the river Dyfi.

To the end of his days he could not look on the waters that covered his kingdom without sorrow. But his greatest grief, he would say, was on that first morning after the disaster. It was so great that he could not speak. Instead he uttered so heart-felt a sigh over the waters that to this day when men would describe a deep sigh of sorrow they call it:

> *The sigh of Gwyddno Garanhir*
> *When the wave rolled over his land.*

III
Baglan the Builder

———————————— ❖ ————————————

There is a tale told of Baglan that when he was a young man, and newly arrived in this land from Brittany, he became a disciple of St Illtud. One day when the saint was cold and in need of a fire, Baglan fetched him glowing coals in the skirt of his cloak, without singeing a thread of it. This was miracle enough for the wise Illtud, and as soon as his hands were warm he presented Baglan with a brass-handled crook [*baglan*, a crook], informing him at the same time that the virtue of the crook was such that it would lead his footsteps to a place where he must build himself a church and become a saint in his turn.

'How shall I know that place when I reach it?' asked Baglan.

'Because you will find there a tree bearing three kinds of fruit,' the saint instructed him, 'and it is unlikely that you will encounter anything on the way to confuse with it.'

Baglan headed south, his boots following the crook, and as he walked three-footed through Glamorgan he saw a tree with a litter of pigs at the roots of it, a hive of bees in the trunk of it, and a nest full of crows in its branches. This was token enough for the wise Baglan, and he at once surveyed the site with an eye to a church. The tree, he saw, grew on a steep slope ill-suited for building, but not far away stretched a smooth and level plain, and it was there that he dug his foundations and began to raise the walls. After these labours he slept with unusual soundness till sunrise, when he found the walls tumbled on the ground and the foundations filling with water. After an even heavier day's work restoring his handiwork he slept even more soundly the second night; but when he looked around him at dawn his walls were if anything flatter and his trenches fuller and wetter. A third time he laboured and a third time he slept, and a third time he awoke to find his work undone. This was hint enough to the wise Baglan that he must be building in the wrong place, and before the crows could squall or the piglets squeal he went back to the tree and began all over again.

Each day as he laboured the crows brought him crusts and the bees yielded honey. The pigs' help was of another kind: with their snouts they hollowed out the new foundations. So Baglan kept their tree within the walls, with a low hatch for the root-dwellers, a window halfway up for the bees, and a hole in the roof for the black squawkers to come in and get out. While the church was building and after it was finished, each animal, bird, and bee would fall silent while Baglan prayed to God above, and the saint loved them and blessed them and commended them to the protection of Heaven. A fine sight it must have been to see them all working and praying and resting together through the seasons of the year, and finest of all when the crows would be perching all over him, and the bees a sunny halo round his holy head, and Baglan himself with his brass-handled crook scratching the back of the big white boar, and the boar grunting out praises to the Maker and Father of all, and prayers in the hearts of each one, till the day came for them to leave the world and be forgotten of men, save for the crook and some stones on the hillside and a story as simple as this.

IV

A Harp on the Water

———— ❖ ————

Long long ago, when the tally of years was at its start in this Island, there was a most wicked king living in a stone palace where the lake of Bala is now. Of him it was said: 'Whom he would kill he killed; whom he would spare he spared', and of these latter it was added that they were extremely few.

One day, not long after he came to the throne, and was still a young man, he was walking in his garden meditating cruelty when a voice, between a silver bell and a bird cry, fell upon his ear, saying: 'Vengeance will come. Vengeance will come.' Almost immediately he heard a second voice, farther off than the first, asking: 'When will it come? When will it come?' Then he heard the first voice reply: 'In the third generation. The third generation.' At this he laughed aloud and shouted through the garden: 'If it shall not come before that who am I to care?' And he planned to be wickeder than ever.

Years later, when his three sons were born and showing signs of being crueller than he, he was once more walking in the garden when he heard the same voices crying the same words: 'Vengeance will come. When will it come? In the third generation, the third generation.' Once more he burst out laughing. 'I defy vengeance,' he shouted. 'And where is there a king mighty enough to wreak it?' And he hurried back indoors to instruct his sons in further wickedness.

Years passed, till the day when the stone walls of the palace rang with rejoicing over the birth of a son to the king's son and heir. A command went out, and armed men to bear it, far and wide through the countryside, ordering all who loved the king (and their own necks too) to proceed to the palace and rejoice with the loudest. In particular a guard was sent after a white-headed harper who lived high up in the hills, that he should provide music for feasting and dancing that night. He came unwillingly and was dumb-dazed to see the silver candle-sticks and goblets of gold, the flow of white mead and the embroidered robes of the ladies. Nor had he much heart for playing as he watched the faces of the oppressors, with their hard, enamelled smiles and ice-filmed eyes. But, 'Play!' ordered the king, and play he must, while the red mouths moved in the white faces and the bedecked hands stabbed like daggers.

Towards midnight there was an interval between feasting and dancing, and the harpist was left alone, without bite or swallow, in a quiet corner overlooking the garden. Suddenly he heard a voice, plangent as a harpstring, and then low thrilling words by his ear: 'Vengeance will come. Vengeance will come.' He turned, and outside in the moonlit garden he could see a small brown bird which hovered and fluttered and seemed to invite him to follow. Stiff and tired as he was, he rose and left the palace, and still the bird withdrew before him, sometimes aloft in the air and sometimes trailing its wing along the path he should take. At the palace wall he stood hesitating, but, 'Vengeance, vengeance!' cried the brown bird, motioning with its head and wings, and it now seemed no easier to return than go forward. On they went, over field and furrow, till the hillside soared before them. Even in his anxiety the harpist could see that the bird directed him by the smoothest way, and always when he paused its cry impelled him forward again. At last they reached the top of the hill, where his exhaustion was so great that he sank to the ground to rest: and now for the first time the bird was silent. The moon slid behind a black cloud that climbed out of the east; instead of a wide vision he could hardly see his hand before him; and the splashing of a brook somewhere below warned him that it might be dangerous for him to make any move. It came into his head and heart how foolish he had been to follow the voice of a bird, and he remembered with dismay that he had left his harp behind him in the palace. 'I must return,' he cried, 'before the dancing starts!' But the thought of those cruel faces struck him with such horror that he could not move, and soon weariness and the dark overcame him and he slept heavily till break of day.

In the morning he arose and rubbed the sleep from his eyes. Then he rubbed them again and again, for when he looked towards the palace there was no palace there: only a huge, calm lake where walls and towers had been, and his harp floating towards him on the face of the waters.

V

The Man Who Killed his Greyhound

❖

So long ago that we are not sure when, there lived a lord at Abergarwan who had a wife and only son. So young was the son that he was still an infant in cradle. The lord of Abergarwan had a hound too, big and faithful, and it was the quality of the hound that it was never unleashed on a beast that it did not kill. One day, when his wife had gone to her devotions, and he himself was taking the air in his yard, he heard the blast of a horn, and after the blast he saw a spent stag going by, and after the stag there came dogs and huntsmen, both afoot and on horse. 'I will go after them,' he said, 'for I am lord of this land and a share of the stag is mine.' The hound would have followed him, but he pointed to the cradle where the child lay sleeping, and the hound lay down at its side.

He had not been absent long when a wolf walked in at the door. It made straight for the cradle, for it wished to devour the child. But the hound rose up, bristling his back, and for two heartbeats they stared at each other. The next moment their jaws locked in battle.

The wolf was leader of his pack, a grey-felled warrior known throughout the mountains, and the smell of his prey haunted his nostrils. The adversaries tore with their teeth and slashed with their claws, till their muzzles dripped red and their pelts hung in tatters. From one side of the room they dragged their way to the other, so that the cradle was overturned and the blankets splashed with blood. But all the time the child lay silent, asleep and unfrightened by the snarls and growls and rattling toenails of those mortal foes; and there was no moment when the wolf might get near him. Then the snarls died to gasps and the growls to hoarse whistles as the hound fought the wolf into the farthest corner, and there in time with the last of his strength tore the red throat out of him.

A little later the man returned, and when he heard his master's footstep in the yard, the hound rose to his feet and dragged himself out to meet him, wagging his tail and trying to lick his hands. But what his master saw was the reeking maw and bloodstained feet, the blood on the floor and the upturned cradle, and no sign or sound of his infant son. 'Monster!' he cried, snatching at his sword; and in a blackness of hate and the belief that the hound had devoured his child, he thrust him through and killed him. Hardly had the dog breathed his last when he heard a cry from the cradle. He rushed towards it and pulled it upright, and there was his son safe and sound, his unstained fingers thrusting the silk sheet from before his mouth. He drew him to his breast, and it was then that he saw the carcass of the wolf in the far corner of the room. He went back to the dog, and saw how his sides were ripped and mangled in that awful struggle, and grief pierced his heart like a thrice-whetted spear.

But what must be will be, nor could all his tears and breast-beating restore his hound to life. He told a bard to make a story of his haste and folly, and the dog he had buried in a high place like a hero. The grave is long lost but the story remains, with a proverb which grew out of it for those who act in haste and repent at leisure: 'As sorry as the man who killed his greyhound.'

VI
The Sun of Llanfabon

——— ❖ ———

In the days that are old and golden, Llanwonno church had a silver bell whose tongue splashed chimes of praises all over the land. None had more liking for its luscious jangle than the big-eared men of Llanfabon, and one night an assembly of them trod splay-footed through the river Taff to steal or (as they would prefer to say) to borrow it, knell, shell and clanger. It was necessary to complete the borrowing before sunrise, for at first light they might look to be observed and pursued by their big-eyed neighbours of Llanwonno.

Behold them then, late into the night, descending the stone-spangled slope of the Taff, their fretwork boots going crash-crash on the pebbles and their poles banging fireworks off the rocks. The bell alone was silent, for they had wound the clapper in velvet and straw before enfolding the whole sonorous dome in a cocoon of scarlet flannel nightshirts. However, just as they were crossing the river, the moon bolted out from behind cloud, alarming them greatly, for they mistook it for the sun. Their arms turned to jelly and they let the bell fall slap into a deep pool. It sank gurgling from sight, and not a note has been heard from it since.

But that is why the big-eyed men of Llanwonno call the moon the sun of Llanfabon, and the big-eared, bugle-nosed, barge-booted men of Llanfabon (who tell the whole story backwards) call the sun the moon of Llanwonno.

VII
Red-hat Otter

———— ❖ ————

One fine day, not so very long ago, two friends set off to hunt otters on the banks of the river Pennant in Merioneth. They were still at a distance from the river when they saw some small, low creature of a red colour running briskly over the meadow ahead of them. Without a word or a wink they gave chase, but before they could overtake it, it reached the river bank and slipped under the roots of a big tree there and was hidden from their sight. For a time they stood pondering and wondering. It couldn't be a squirrel and it couldn't be a stoat or a fox, so they decided that it must be an otter. Now an otter with a red coat was a treasure unknown and undreamt-of, so they determined to catch it alive, and one of them went off to the nearest farm to borrow a sack for the purpose. Meantime his companion carefully examined the tree roots.

When the first man returned, he was able to inform him that there were only two holes under the roots, the one facing landwards (into which the otter had run) and the other adjoining the river. So while the one held the sack over the mouth of the river hole, the other thrust his staff into the other hole, to drive the creature forward. In no time at all something came out and fell plop into the sack. Immensely pleased with themselves (for they looked to become famous as the men who captured a red otter), the two hunters left their day's sport and set off for home, one of them carrying the staffs and the other the sack over his shoulder. Judge of their surprise when before they had crossed a single meadow they heard a voice speak out of the sack: 'My mother is calling me. Must she come and fetch me?'

They dropped the sack as though it had burned them, and as it lay on the ground a wriggle went through it, its mouth was lifted, and a red cotton cap with a head inside peeped forth. Then out popped a tiny man whose jacket and breeches were red, and his shoes too, and off he went at a run towards the river where some bushes swallowed him up, looking just like a red otter again. However, this time the two hunters thought they would do wisely to go on home and meddle no more with the fair small folk, nor is it recorded that they ever hunted that part of the river again or saw the little red man on its bank or knew the sharp-edged blessing of meeting the little man's mother, whoever she might be.

VIII
Cadwalader and All His Goats

———— ❖ ————

There was once a hill-farmer named Cadwalader who owned a large herd of goats, the finest of which was called Jenny. No goat was ever so handsome of a week-end as she, for the fair small folk combed her free of her tangles each Friday, and on holiday-eves besides. As for her good sense, it was Cadwalader's view that there were few among goats or humans to equal her. No wonder then that he grew so fond of her, or that she appeared equally fond of him.

But as every dog will have his day, so will every goat. Jenny must have thought as much, surely, for one summer evening she showed him her heels and bolted up the mountain. Instantly he gave chase, at first calling on her with promises, then with threats, until at last he had no breath to spare for anything except the business of running. The slopes were steep and the paths rough, and whenever he drew close to her tail, Jenny leapt from rock to crag and then to rock again, and left him looking silly. There was something so deliberate about the way she did this that he grew in a rage with her, nor was his temper improved by the stones that blued his feet and blacked his legs, or the sousing streams and dousing water-falls. Finally he found himself on a narrow ledge with a second ledge opposite and a drip-drop chasm between. Coolly confronting him was Jenny, and he knew by her eye that when he took one more step she would spring over the chasm and leave him gasping worse than ever.

'I could forgive you,' he panted, 'for breaking my leg, but I will never forgive you for making me look such a fool.' And as she sprang for the far side he let fly at her with a stone and hit her in full flight, so that a loud scream came out of her and she fell to the rocks below.

Painfully he descended to where she lay, his rage already melted to grief and pity. She was still breathing, but only just, and as he touched her she lifted her head and licked his hand.

'Jenny,' he cried, 'what have I done to you? Can you ever forgive me?'

Tears splashed from his eyes and from Jenny's too as he sat down beside her and drew her head on his lap. Soon it grew dark but he sat on, stroking and kissing her hair, and feeling her grow quieter and quieter.

Then in one moment of time the moon broke clear of the mountain and shone down upon them, and to his astonishment he found that Jenny had become transformed into a beautiful young woman with silken hair and soft brown eyes, and that far from being numbered among the dead or dying, she was looking as pleased with herself as a cat that laps cream. But if this surprised him (and surprise him it did), what surprised him still more was to hear her speak these words most tenderly: 'Ah, my Cadwalader,' she sighed, 'have I found you then at last?'

Now Cadwalader was far from certain that he wanted to be found, at least in this kind of way. Nor could he decide whether he should still call her Jenny, and he was getting pins and needles into the bargain. So he was well content when she stood up and, having taken his hand in hers, set off nimbly up the mountain. Not that her hand left him content for long. It was soft, there was no doubt about that, and it had the usual thumb and four fingers; yet it felt just like a hoof all the time. And though she talked to him the whole way with a tenderness which he found quite alarming, there was a tremulous bleat in her voice which alarmed him even more. 'There is no question of it,' he told himself, watching her white feet skip among the rocks, 'I am in a bad place already, and heading for a worse.'

A few minutes later he saw how right he had been, for he and Jenny-that-was arrived on a wide shelf of rock on top of the mountain, where they were instantly surrounded by a huge flock of goats. He had never seen such beards and horns, and never heard such bleating. But Jenny thrust her way through them, talking now in Goat and now in Human, till they arrived in front of the biggest billy-goat of them all. She at once did him such reverence as one does to a king.

'Is this the man?' asked king Billy.

'It is,' she replied.

'Hm,' said the king, 'I expected something better. Even for a human, he looks a poor specimen to me.'

'He will look different *after*,' she assured him.

'After what?' wondered Cadwalader, but he kept the thought to himself.

'And now,' asked king Billy, turning his red-rimmed eyes on Cadwalader, 'do you take this Jenny to be your lawful wedded nanny?'

'Of course,' thought Cadwalader, 'they mean after I am turned into a goat. No wonder she said I would look different!'

'No, your majesty,' he gasped out. 'I don't want to be a goat or have anything more to do with goats.'

'Not want to be a goat!' roared king Billy. 'Miserable mortal that you are, it is we lords of creation who want nothing more to do with you!' And for all Jenny's despairing bleat as she saw herself left on the shelf, he rushed at Cadwalader and with one tremendous butt of his billy-bully horns knocked him clean off the mountain.

It was morning when Cadwalader found himself lying with his head in a bush and his feet in a bog and the mountain bending over him. The sun was shining and there were birds flirting nimbly in Heaven, but all Cadwalader wanted was to get back home. Needless to say, he never saw his Jenny again in any shape or form. Not that this greatly mattered, for he had now so lost his taste for goats that he sold the entire herd and kept sheep instead, and if there were another story to tell of him (which there isn't), it would probably be called 'Cadwalader and All His Sheep'.

THE SALT WELSH SEA

———— ❖ ————

Once in a coloured summer, when the sea was still fresh water (and women were women and fish were fish), there were three brothers born in a yellow-washed house on the long Welsh Tramping Road. When they grew up, Glyn ploughed the land and Lyn ploughed the sea, but Maldwyn, who was the youngest, ploughed only his own furrow. As a result Glyn prospered and ate honey on his bread, and Lyn prospered and ate apples with his cheese, but Maldwyn and his wife walked the tired highways and shared their emptiness between them, in fair shares. But whenever on their journeyings they passed the yellow-washed house they would call and ask for a gift, till Glyn's righteous nose grew sick of the smell of them.

'I know the thing I'll do,' he told himself at last, 'that I may be rid of them for ever. Little brother,' he asked Maldwyn, 'what would you promise for me to give you a little pig all to yourself?'

'Anything you ask, kind brother. Anything you ask.'

'Your word is your word, so here is your little pig, and now, little brother, do you go immediately to Blazes.'

'My word is my word,' agreed Maldwyn, 'so if you will

call off your dog who is biting my leg, I shall trouble you no further.'

All that day they walked up and down in the land, with the little pig on a string behind them, looking for Blazes. Towards nightfall they came to the lighted door of a cottage called Cartref [Home], and saw a hoary-headed man walking in the garden in the cool of the twilight hour, with a long white beard on him, and the look of a shepherd to his trews and jerkin.

'Good evening,' they said politely. 'Would you by any chance be Blazes?'

'On the contrary,' said the old man. 'I have hardly a friend in the world. But if you are looking for Mr Blazes, why, he is a very old acquaintance of mine, and you are sure to find him in the house called Fernal down at the bottom of the valley. A roast on the spit is his greatest pleasure, and I can't help thinking that when he sees your little pig he will be all over you to buy it. But if you will take my advice, my dears, don't let it go save in exchange for the handmill which stands behind his kitchen door. It is the quality of this handmill that it grinds out what you will, neither slowly nor exceeding small; and if you should pass this way as you come back, I shall be very glad to show you the knack of it.'

They thanked him and walked down through the shadows of the valley till they reached the big house Fernal, and gave a rattling ta-ra-ra on Mr Blazes' door. It opened on the instant, and there were Mr Blazes' friends and servants, some hooking them inside and some poking the fire with their noses and some already testing the plumpness of the little pig, the water splashing off their tongues as they did so. Mr Blazes instantly offered him a cool thousand in years for the pig.

'A thousand thanks in exchange,' said Maldwyn, 'and for your warm welcome too. But my wife and I have saved up for a twelvemonth and a day that we might have this little pig for our Christmas dinner, and it is midsummer already. And yet,' he added when his wife nudged him, 'because I am the softest-hearted man alive, and bat-blind to my own interest, to save you from disappointment I will give you the pig free and gratis in exchange for the handmill behind your kitchen door.'

But for a long while Mr Blazes would not hear of it. Instead he offered Maldwyn his heart's desire, a seat in the government, ratbane for his less popular relations, and hair for the bald patch on his crown. But, 'I love my relations,' protested Maldwyn, and, 'It's not baldness, it's the way the light falls,' simpered his wife; and the handmill it must be or nothing.

By this time the floor was slippery with slaver, and the servants were howling out, 'Pig! Give us pig! Pig or we perish!' so Mr Blazes had to change his mind and give them the handmill after all. Throughout these proceedings, the little pig had been keeping pretty close to Maldwyn and his wife, and you can guess how he squealed when he found himself tucked inside Mr Blazes' elbow.

Back up the road they went till they found the hoary-headed man with the long white beard, who smiled as he gave them instructions how to start the handmill and, better still, how to stop it once it had started. They could hardly wait till they got down by the sea and set the handmill grinding. First it ground out a house for them, and then candles to light it, and a table and chairs, and meat and drink and bedclothes galore, 'Really,' they said, 'this going to Blazes is quite a good sort of thing!' And finally they had it grind them out a brand-new cockerel with gilded spurs and a scarlet comb, so that they might be wakened early in the morning and start it grinding again.

In this agreeable fashion they lived till the wheat harvest, when they ground themselves a feast, and Maldwyn drove up to the yellow-washed house in a carriage-and-four and invited his brother Glyn (the one who ploughed the land) to take a bite with them. He came, his eyes round as teapots, and brought the neighbours with him, and they were dumb-dazed to see the wines and snuff and the plates of gold and cups of white sea-ivory. 'Only yesterday they lacked a penny to scratch with, and now they are wealthier than milk-vendors or kings. Little brother,' he begged, 'where in Blazes did you get all this wealth?'

'From behind the kitchen door,' said Maldwyn, with equal truth and wariness, and not another word could Glyn drag out of him till the neighbours had all gone home. But Glyn stayed on and plied him with drink and flattery, till in the end he told him everything about the mill except how to stop it grinding. And when Maldwyn fell into the cinders and snored, his brother laid hold on the handmill and staggered off with it to the yellow-washed house.

'Wife,' he said in the morning, 'I should like you to go down to the oat-field by the sea, and cut the first swathe. For once I'm thinking to take the dinner into my own charge.'

As soon as she was out of the house, he lifted the handmill on to the table and regarded it lovingly. 'First,' he told himself, 'let it grind me out maids to set and serve the great feast I am thinking to give. And if they are comely maids, why, so much the better.' He rapped on his beer-barrel and it was nearly empty. 'And beer too,' he thought, 'till my barrel runneth over.' And then he spoke aloud to the handmill:

> *'Little mill, little mill,*
> *Grind me maids and ale;*
> *Little mill, little mill,*
> *Grind them dark and pale.'*

No sooner had the words left his mouth than a dark girl was wafted forth on a wave of strong drink, and then a pale one, and then a tawny one, and then a white and a brown and a yellow, and the ale rising a foot deep throughout the house.

'Enough,' he shouted, 'I said enough! Stop, mill, stop now, will you, hi!' But the handmill went on grinding, and soon there they were, all swimming about for dear life, till the beer burst out at the doors and windows and went roaring and foaming down to the sea. It found Glyn's wife in its path, and she took hardly a swallow before she was off the land and into the deep, with her husband and his maids about her. The maids stayed happy as mice in hay, for they knew none but a moist element, but Glyn and his wife soon touched rock-bottom, and there they stayed without a bubble rising.

From his house along the bay Maldwyn heard and saw the commotion, and he felt he need look no farther for who had stolen his mill. So he climbed up on to the green hill behind the yellow-washed house and ordered the mill to stop grinding out first maids and then ale, and once the flood had subsided he carried it back to his own place. He had it grind him gold slates, so that his house would shine fair and far over the Welsh sea.

The very next week his brother Lyn (the one who ploughed the sea) came sailing into the bay on his red-masted ship with a cargo of salt. He was surprised—but not ill-pleased—to find the water smelling of ale and full of mermaids, and lost a couple of men overboard in no time. He soon learned the fate of the yellow-washed house, and, his eyes round as port-holes, came a-visiting to his brother Maldwyn's. 'Only yesterday they lacked a penny to scratch with, and now they are wealthier than deep-sea lawyers or admirals. Little brother,' he begged, 'where in Blazes did you get all this wealth?'

'From behind the kitchen door,' replied Maldwyn; but his brother plied him with drink and flattery till in the end he told him everything about the mill except how to stop it grinding.

'Will it grind salt?' asked Lyn.

'To make all the oceans briny,' Maldwyn assured him.

Lyn said nothing to this, but all the time he was thinking what a fine stroke it would be to a poor sea-captain to own the mill and grind out salt and no longer go long voyages through storm and wrack to fetch his cargoes. And when his brother fell into the cinders and snored, he laid hold on the handmill and staggered off with it to his red-masted ship, and they at once set sail, and when they were well out in Cardigan Bay he set the handmill lovingly on deck and said:

'Little mill, little mill,
Grind me salty salt;

Little mill, little mill,
Grind it without halt.'

And at these words the mill ground out salt till it lay like snow over the deck and the crew climbed the red mast to get out of its way. But the higher they climbed (and Lyn climbed highest of all), the higher it climbed after them, and in the fullness of time, what with the fullness of salt, the ship touched rock-bottom and all the crew were pickled.

Not long afterwards the hoary-headed man with the long white beard passed that way on the long Welsh Tramping Road. He saw the mermaids in the water and tasted the salt in the sea. 'Truly,' he said, 'I move in a mysterious way my wonders to perform.' And because it seemed good to him, he left the mermaids there, and the handmill too, and it keeps grinding away to this day, and that is why the seas around Wales are salter than most seas and, as we all know, growing salter.

HIGH EDEN

---------- ❖ ----------

A year before a year (and for years before that) a man and his wife lived in the turf-roofed cottage with the black tarred door where the long Welsh Tramping Road leads up from Fernal to the mansions of High Eden. The man was named Jonah and his wife Elen, and it must be admitted before we go any farther that Jonah looked blacker than his door to the gooseberry eyes of the neighbours. But Elen was a tidy old soul enough, and for the years of her lifetime thought herself not too badly treated by the world while they shared bed and board and draughts from the door and window. And so things might have continued, from that day to this, had not Jonah dreamed one night that he stood beneath a purple vault and heard a red voice roar in welcome: 'Now you are come home, Jonah. Now you are come home!' He heard his own voice next, thin as a sparrow's. 'Home where?' it was pleading. 'Tell me that, home where?' Then the red voice roared again: 'Home to Blazes, Jonah. Where else but to Blazes?' At which he was so frightened that he heard the flesh rustle on his bones and floated clean out of bed on his wave of cold sweat.

'Elen, dear wife,' he told her, once he had fetched himself

upright and recounted his dream, 'Powers and Majesties have discoursed to me this night, and I suspect I shall soon be no more. Wretch that I am, I am frozen with fright to think of the Fernal bonfire, so promise me, Elen, please promise me, that you will see my soul safe into the Other Place. And yet,' he ended despairingly, 'they will be slow to slip an old otter like me into the salmon pools of High Eden.'

'Jonah,' she comforted him, 'you are no white lamb, to be sure, but you shall be nobody's black sheep if I can help it, neither.' And she promised that she would see his soul into High Eden though the cat should bark and the sky rain glass splinters.

For a week and a day Elen sat by Jonah's bedside, waiting. All this time she was holding a strong leather bag in front of his face, and when finally he gave up the ghost it huddled into the bag with a tired sigh and she tied up the neck of it with a leathern thong. His soul was a good deal heavier than she had expected of a man so short that he could milk the cows standing up; but she was never one to sit moping, so in a minute or two she slung the sack over her shoulder and walked out to the Tramping Road. First she looked down through the shadows of the valley to the smoking chimneys of the house Fernal, but there came an anxious wriggle from inside the sack, and she turned her face instead towards the hills and blue roofs of High Eden.

She had been walking for an hour and a minute when a man met her, standing at the roadside by a new-fallen bridge, his face blackish, and with smoke blowing out of his nose.

'In my dark name,' said the man, 'give me what is mine of Jonah's soul, or you shall go no farther.'

But when he reached out his hot hand all he got from Elen was a cool palm. 'Surely, lord Blazes,' she told him, 'you know that I was Jonah's better half, so why grow so heated after the worse? Tell me now, what would be a fair price for throwing a bridge over the pit?'

Mr Blazes snapped his fingers till they sparked. 'I have too much at stake, Elen,' he warned her, 'to play for glass marbles. But if the first living thing to cross it shall be mine, a bridge there shall be, and pronto.'

'Pronto it is,' said Elen gamely. They struck hands on their bargain, and when the bridge called Pronto spanned the pit before her she blew notes on her willow-wood whistle till Jonah's golden heeling-dog ran up and she motioned him across it.

'Well,' the architect admitted, 'you were too clever for me that time, old Elen. But give Mr Blazes his due, he never rats on a bargain.' He dipped negligently down, but the fox-headed, white-toothed corgi, who cared not a straw for man or devil and was excited by the word *rats*, snapped him once, twice, thrice, till his hands were all running with fire. 'To Heaven with your corgi!' he shouted in a rage, and the very next moment he wasn't there. The corgi sniffed in a puzzled way at the leathern bag, then swaggered off home, and Elen, between a chuckle and a groan, crossed the devil's bridge on her way to High Eden.

When she arrived at the blue-roofed mansions she found a narrow door to knock on, and when she had knocked only once, a man came bustling out who she knew by his keys was Saint Peter.

'Good-day, Blessed Peter,' she greeted him politely. 'I have come here with the soul of Jonah my husband. I expect you will have heard of him, poor fellow that he was, and it is my errand to ask you to take him into High Eden.'

Peter shook his head somewhat quickly. 'None by the name of Jonah was ever much good, and your Jonah was surely the fishiest of them. I have a charge-sheet on him as long as my left wing. No, no, my good woman, I am sorry, but High Eden is not for the like of your Jonah.'

'And yet,' said Elen, none too sweetly, 'bad as he was, he never denied his Lord thrice in one night before the cock crowed.'

She would have enlarged on this theme had not Peter, looking a shade pink, stepped back inside and closed the door in her face.

For a minute or two she stood sighing and mumbling, the bag grown heavier on her back, but when she had recovered her breath she knocked again on the door, and when she had knocked twice a man came earnestly out who she knew by his scripts and his screeds was Saint Paul.

'Good-day, Blessed Paul,' she greeted him warmly. 'It is nice to see you safe after your shipwreck. I have come here with the soul of Jonah my husband. Perhaps you haven't heard of him, but he wasn't as bad as some I could name, and it is my errand to ask you to take him into High Eden.'

'Jonah?' mused Paul, tapping his teeth with a blue pencil. 'You must excuse me, I am very bad at names. Oh,' he said, '*that* Jonah!' He shook his head reprovingly. 'Why, we have a file on him as long as a harpstring, and I have still longer been planning to pen him one of my Epistles. No, no, my good woman, I am sorry, I wish it were otherwise, but High Eden is not for the like of your Jonah.'

'And yet,' retorted Elen, none too gently, 'I should have expected you to be good at names, Paul who was also Saul. My Jonah, ripe though he was for our Master's pruning-hook, never breathed out threatenings and slaughter against the Lord, nor, being exceedingly mad, did he persecute them unto strange cities.'

She would have continued reciting Scripture to good purpose had not Paul, looking a shade red, stepped back inside and slammed the door in her face.

The good old wife stood there a long while afterwards sighing and grieving. The bag on her back had now grown so heavy and so agitated that she feared she would not have the strength to carry it much longer; but finally she made up her mind to try once again and knocked on the door, and when she had knocked three times the door opened, and before her stood One who by the marks of the nails and the thorns she knew was Christ Himself; our Saviour.

'Blessed Saviour,' she said humbly, 'I will tell you the truth, without any lie. I have brought here the soul of Jonah my husband, who next to me was the most worthless of Thy creatures. By Thy goodness, not his, I hope he may enter High Eden.'

'I heard your promise, Elen,' said the Saviour, 'and I know your faith. But tell me, have you tried Peter? Have you tried Paul? It is they who write the records and balance our accounts.'

Our Saviour's words lay heavy on the heart of Elen, even heavier than the bag that bowed her curved back.

'Besides,' He continued, 'I am told that this Jonah of yours was a man of great sins and little faith.'

'So great and so little,' said Elen weeping, 'that only Thou canst bring him past the door.'

'Believe me, Elen,' said our Saviour gently, 'this is not in My hands.'

He turned away slowly, so slowly, and Elen's heart would have broken in two had not her thoughts been impelled by these last words to her own hands and what was in *them*: and that was the neck of the bag that held her husband's soul. Suddenly it seemed to her that the whole wide hall of Heaven pealed its welcome through the slowly shutting door, and slipping the bag from her shoulder she slung it whirling in an arc far, far, far, into the blue and sunny hollow. And with the closing of the starry door behind the soul of Jonah, a stone rolled from off her heart; her feet, which had been heavy as hammers, grew light as egg-shells, and she set off downhill for the turf-roofed cottage with the black tarred door which was her home for some years yet awhile. Jonah's golden heeling-dog she kept till the end of his days, and after what Mr Blazes said we need not be surprised that he walked close behind her when again she crossed the bridge of Pont-y-Pronto and fared by the long Welsh Tramping Road in the fullness of time to the blue-roofed many mansions of High Eden.

Pronouncing the Names

———— ❖ ————

At first sight some Welsh names look hard to pronounce. In fact they are easy, much easier than English. The following rules will lead to a reasonably accurate pronunciation of all the names in this book.

I. The stress in Welsh names usually falls on the last syllable but one. In the names that follow it is indicated by a syllable in italics.

II. c is the sound k, as in English cat; g is the sound g in gun; f is the English v. Thus Cigfa is pronounced [*Kig*va].

r is always rolled, and h is always aspirated strongly.

dd is the th sound in English breathe; ll is the famous Welsh 'double l', somewhat like the tl in little, especially if that word is spoken forcibly. Thus Lludd is pronounced [*Llea*the].

ch is the sound we all know in Scottish loch.

III. All Welsh vowels are pure sounds.

a can be short, as in cat (so *Bran*wen), or long, as in father, e.g. Brân [Brahn].

e can be short, as in pen, or long, like French è. The short sound is the commoner. Thus Llefelys [Lle*vel*is].

i can be short, as in pin, or long, as in machine. Iddawg [E*eth*owg].

w when a vowel has the short sound of oo in book or the long sound of oo in boon. Twrch Trwyth [Toorch Trooith], Matholwch [Math*o*looch], Cadw [*Kad*oo], Culhwch [roughly K*il*hooch].

u has a short sound, something like the i in pin, and a long sound, something like the i in machine. Clud [roughly Kleed].

y has three sounds, one short like the i in pin, one short like the u in pun, one long like the i in machine. Cynddylig [Kun*thull*ig], Ysbaddaden [Usbath*a*den], Llŷr [Lleer], Rhonabwy [Rhonabwee].

ei, eu, ey are pronounced like the y in English why; and ae is similar. Cei [Ky], Blodeuwedd [Blod*eye*weth], Teyrnon [T*yre*non].

aw is similar to ow in English cow. Gwawl [Gwowl], Lleu Llaw Gyffes [Lly Llow *Guffes*].

As a final guide the more important names in the first story in the book *Pwyll and Pryderi*, are pronounced thus: Pwyll [Pooill], Pryderi [Prud*der*ee], Rhiannon [Rhee*ann*on].